A LAND WITHOUT MERCY

A Land
Without Mercy

Alan Lacey

NEW ENGLISH LIBRARY
TIMES MIRROR

TO LYNETTE DOBSON
WITH BEST WISHES FOR THE FUTURE

An NEL Original
© New English Library, 1974

*

FIRST NEL PAPERBACK EDITION MAY 1974

NEL Books are published by
New English Library Limited from Barnard's Inn, Holborn, London, E.C.1.
Made and printed in Great Britain by Hunt Barnard Printing Ltd., Aylesbury, Bucks.

45001817 2

AUTHOR'S NOTE

This is the story of a man, and it is dedicated to realism. Set in the period when the legends of Arthur were originated in real life, the story concerns the distortion, corruption and the eventual destruction of a man's personality and his way of life.

When I sat down to write this book, I had two things in mind: historical accuracy and creating a story and characters which readers can identify with, a story which, in a nutshell, is real. To put it another way, the romance happens as romance happens in real life and the fighting and the living done as it was in the time of Arthur, or rather Artus.

People tend to believe that everyone lives from day to day until they die with the same personality, the same principles and that if one strives hard enough to achieve what he or she wants then all will be well in the end. I have attempted to show the innermost feelings of a man with his life collapsing constantly around him. His reactions to circumstances and the people who cause them to arise. His reactions to love and hate. I have attempted to show the facts of life, which come together to say that all will not be fine at the end.

A.R.L.

GLOSSARY OF PLACE-NAMES

The period that this book deals with is shortly after the final collapse of Roman rule in Britain. During this period, most places still kept the names given to them by the Romans and these remained largely unchanged until foreign invaders over the centuries of history altered them.

The names given in ITALICS are those of the Author's invention and are given here to assist the reader in understanding and interpreting the travels of the characters.

PLACE	IDENTIFICATION
Aquae Sulis	Bath
Armorica	Brittany
"Blackhorse country"	Part of Britain held by Artus, mainly borderland
Camboglanna	Birdoswold, Hadrian's Wall
Calaractonium	Catterick
CEORL'S CAMP	about 16 miles west of Water Newton (Durobrivae)
Danum	Doncaster
Durobrivae	Water Newton, Hunts.
DYFAN'S CAMP	6 miles west of Ancaster
Gaul	France
Glien	River Glen, Lincs.
Glevum	Gloucester
Lavatrae	Bowes, Yorks.
Lindum	Lincoln
Olicana	Ilkley, Yorks.
THE VILLA	About 10 miles east of Ancaster

The personal names Artus, Bedwyr, Cai, Mordrawt, Winifred, Agrippa and Wlanca are better known as: Arthur, Sir Bedevere, Sir Kay, Mordred, Guenevere, Sir Aggravane and Sir Lancelot.

PROLOGUE

We found him lying face down in the mud, sprawled across the track leading up to the encampment. His mop of red hair contrasted sharply with the grass and the foliage of the surrounding trees which marched up the embankment to the left and stumbled downhill to the right.

Pedr approached him first, sword in hand. The man made no move but lay motionless on the track. A light, hazy drizzle matted his hair. Pedr bent over him and laid his sword down at his side on the ground. He lowered himself to one knee and rolled the body over onto his back. He put his ear to the man's chest. 'Saxon,' Pedr reported, lifting his head. 'And alive.' He stood up, picking up his sword and sheathing it.

I walked over to Pedr's side and looked down at the Saxon. 'He's not a warrior. Look at his build. He carries no weapons.'

Pedr nodded in agreement, scrutinizing the man's ragged attire. The Saxon was wrapped in old sheepskins, plastered with the mud from the track, and there was no trace of armour on him. His limbs were spindly and his face was thin and bruised, filthy with the mud too. He looked about twenty winters old, nearly the same age as Pedr and myself. 'I suppose we can take him up to the encampment or run him through because he's a Saxon,' I said sarcastically. Pedr grunted and heaved the man up and slung him over his shoulder. We began the trudge back up the track to the encampment.

CHAPTER ONE

Aonghus

The encampment squatted atop a large, rocky hill that protruded from the surrounding greenery rather incongruously. Pedr carried the Saxon awkwardly over one shoulder, up the track which wound to the top of the hill, and to a gate way in the rough stone wall that surrounded the ancient camp. This was the rear entrance. Here we were confronted by Bledig, a burly Celt with a bushy black beard and hair that served to conceal the contours of the man's face. His eyes, however, were those of a forest animal, brown and darting. As we came nearer, he drew his sword and gestured towards us with it. 'What is this? A Saxon! By the Gods! Step no closer.'

Pedr halted and answered Bledig. 'As you can see, he is harmless, and carries no weapons.'

'You have no right to bring any Saxon into this camp. If he is injured then put him to the sword and have done with it. I fear Ceorl would show less mercy.'

Pedr dropped the Saxon to the ground and pulled out his sword, advancing towards Bledig. 'Get out of my way you son of a cur!' he called and lunged at Bledig with his sword. Bledig stopped the blade with his own. He then took up the assault, but Pedr was the best man with a sword in the camp apart from Ceorl himself. Bledig was soon overwhelmed and forced back inside the gate. Only a few times had their swords actually crossed. We walked in unmolested apart from harsh words hurled at us from the angered Bledig as we made our way to our own hut, Pedr still carrying the Saxon.

I pushed open the door of the hut and Pedr entered with his burden. We were greeted by startled glances from the other occupants, Walwyn, Eiluned, Peneli and Elspeth. Pedr walked to the fire and Walwyn stood up, making room there for Pedr to lay the Saxon down. Walwyn was first to speak: 'Who . . . ?'

Pedr took off his swordbelt and tossed it onto his bed-rugs near the door .'A Saxon, by the looks of him. He's hurt. We found him on the track near the rear gateway.'

'How did he come to be there?' Peneli asked. 'We're

more than three days' ride from Saxon territory.' She seemed worried.

I shut the door and slung off my fur cloak. 'He's not a warrior. He's unarmed.'

'A spy then . . . ?' said Walwyn.

'Perhaps,' I said, and moved to warm my hands over the fire brazier. Eiluned shuffled round to the Saxon and rested his head on her knee. She examined the bruises on his face and looked into the mop of hair. When she withdrew her fingers she found them stained with blood from a wound on the man's head.

'He has received a bad blow on the head,' Eiluned reported. 'But he will mend, if we can stop the blood from flowing out of the wound.'

Peneli stood up and came around to Eiluned's side. 'I will collect some herbs,' she stated. 'I'll prepare them at once.' And with that she withdrew. We sat in silence for a moment, pondering on the events our actions might cause in the near future. We had acted rashly, and now we would learn the consequences.

'Where's Paulus?' I enquired.

'In the longhut in council with Ceorl,' Walwyn said. He sat down and watched Eiluned tend the Saxon. Walwyn was a watcher. He peered through the black curls which overhung his brow, and curled his upper lip up to chew on the hairs of his large moustache.

I went to my sleeping place and sprawled on the rugs to await Peneli's return with the promised concoction.

Elspeth, who had remained silent in her characteristic manner throughout, stood up and emerged from the other side of the fire. 'You don't think that he's a spy, Ailin?' she asked me.

'I didn't say that. I doubt it, that's all.'

'Why?' she persisted. She moved closer to me, her broad hips swaying slightly. I raised myself on my elbow. 'What else could he be?' she asked.

'I don't know,' I said. 'But why has no-one brought word of this? Ceorl would give a reward to the man who caught a Saxon in the act of spying. Perhaps he was cast out by his own kind.'

Elspeth nodded and walked over to Eiluned and looked down on the man's face.

I was about to ask Pedr what he thought Ceorl would do

when the curtain was thrust aside which served for a door and Paulus entered. He was a small man, a little younger than myself, with Roman features and a whispy mat of tawny hair. 'I just heard,' he said. 'There's quite a stir in the longhut. Bledig was hysterical. Ceorl's coming over when he's calmed them all down.'

There were voices from outside and I saw through the open doorway that Bledig had spread the word and a crowd was gathering outside our hut. Their dialogue sounded angry and I was glad that most of the men were either in the longhut or out hunting. I jumped up from my rugs to get a better view of the commotion outside. Paulus stepped out and cleared them from around the doorway. He was about to cover the entrance when the plump figure of Peneli slid through the opening. She carried an earthenware basin containing a dark green paste. Paulus closed the entrance behind her. He did not want anyone intruding while the women cared for the sick Saxon.

Peneli knelt beside Eiluned and transferred the Saxon's head to her own lap. From beneath the various items of clothing she wore, she produced a short knife and with it cut away the hair about the wound. She then thrust the blade of the knife into the brazier and waited for it to glow with heat. When, on inspection, she saw that the blade was red, she asked Pedr to hold the Saxon's shoulders down. Pedr did so and Peneli applied the knife to the wound. The Saxon seemed to wake instantly and screamed in unexpected torment whilst we stood in silence. His body writhed under Pedr's hands. Then the Saxon lapsed again into unconciousness. And just as the last sizzle and tangy smell of burning scalp arose from the tip of the blade, Ceorl strode into the hut forcing open the door and nearly knocking Paulus over.

Peneli withdrew the knife and quietly placed it on the floor beside her. Eiluned gave Ceorl a disapproving glance and then continued to watch Peneli, who was now smearing on the green paste. Ceorl was not a man to talk a great deal. He said nothing, but pushed Peneli aside and raised the Saxon's head by the red hair. The Saxon moaned. Ceorl turned the head and examined the face in the firelight .He then dropped the head and raised himself, turning to face Elspeth, Pedr, Paulus and myself. Pedr had retreated from the fireside when Ceorl entered. Ceorl was the one man in the camp to whom Pedr gave his full respect in the military sense of the word.

'What's he doing here?' Ceorl demanded. Ceorl was tall and well-built for a Celt. He was clean shaven and freckled. His eyes were sunken, small and staring. Like me, Ceorl wore his deep brown, curly hair in a semi-Roman style. His lips were pursed, waiting for the reply.

'We found him lying wounded on the track leading up to the rear gate,' I explained.

'We?'

Pedr said: 'Ailin and I.'

Ceorl frowned. 'Trust you pair of fools to bring the enemy within strangling distance! He isn't staying here. Either put an end to his lousy Saxon life or take him out of the camp and tell him to lose himself in the forest.' Ceorl said no more. He glanced around the faces in the hut, waiting for the response to his command. He looked to the door and saw the faces of the other people of the encampment. All expressions whether from them or ourselves were in awe of Ceorl. No return glare could penetrate the iron-cold gaze he gave. After a short time, that seemed an age, Ceorl pushed his way out of the hut and through the crowd of people which began to disperse.

Anger burned in my throat. 'I won't do either! If the Saxon goes so do I. I'm tired of Ceorl's orders. This man's no more a warrior than me!' I pointed down at the Saxon who began to squirm and moan as sleep vacated his body.

My defiance had not welled up in a moment. It had been waiting a long time to be revealed, and I knew that my friends felt the same way as me.

'Me too,' said Pedr, scratching his head.

'And me,' Eiluned came in. That made me glad, for I had a growing fondness of Eiluned that made me envious of Walwyn, to whom she was betrothed. She boasted of coming from a line of true Romans, a race which I personally held in great esteem. Her facial features showed her ancestry, the colour and texture of her hair also. But her skin was of a healthy white and seemed to me to reflect her elegance and purity. I judged her to be beautiful.

I looked at Paulus. He nodded in response to my gaze. 'I'm with you,' he said and Peneli moved to Pedr's side. It was to Pedr that she was betrothed. Both her and Eiluned wished to marry soon.

Walwyn looked perturbed, almost afraid. I was, of course, biased but in my estimation Walwyn was a coward. People thought the same of me because of my refusal to join in battle but they made the mistake of regarding compassion and forethought as cowardice. If only we could have communicated with the Saxons . . .

Walwyn shook his head. 'Eiluned and I are not leaving.' Eiluned said quietly: 'You speak only for yourself.' Walwyn looked surprised. 'We are betrothed!' he exclaimed.

'We are no longer betrothed if you stay here with Ceorl.'

Walwyn looked blankly at her. His eyes seemed suddenly full of remorse. 'I knew something like this would happen. We weren't meant for each other.' Walwyn left the hut. His pitiful attitude sickened me at first, but I recalled the midsummer festival last year. I saw the fires burning on the hill, the dancing. I remembered being whirled around with Peneli round and round and . . . I remembered the oath of love we swore. I remembered the torchlight and the wild rose, and there seeing Pedr fall beneath her spell. How she enchanted him and discarded me, and how this felt . . . like a dagger in the heart. I found I could forgive Walwyn, then.

During the few heartbeats between the time that memories came and went in my mind, Elspeth agreed to accompany us. The question was now where to go. We considered several other small villages, but could think of no leader who would be willing to accept into his camp a Saxon.

'What about Dyfan's Camp?' Peneli suggested.

Pedr laughed a little. 'No chance. There's no chance with any other of the camps and fortresses in this area. The warriors have seen too much conflict with the Saxons. No chieftain in his right mind would allow a Saxon to sit at his hearth-fire.'

'Artus did,' Elspeth mused. 'Wlanca, prince of Belne in Gaul is of Saxon blood.'

Eiluned seemed to think for a moment very hard. Then she burst out: 'The Villa!'

'What's that?' said Pedr.

'The Villa,' she repeated. 'Do you remember, Elspeth.'

Elspeth thought for a moment and then said: 'Of course! I remember, Eiluned. Your parents' home. It's only two days' ride from here. No-one lives there now.'

'Two days ride in which direction?' Pedr asked.

'Towards the sunrise,' Eiluned replied. I thought that she seemed remarkably undisturbed by the ending of her courtship. Pedr, the realist, was thinking of other things however.

'Towards the sunrise? That's a little too close to the Saxons for my liking.'

'I'd tend to agree.' Paulus said. 'What's the terrain like around this villa? Could it be defended?'

To me the question seemed absurd, but it was a consideration and Paulus knew more of the ways of the warrior than I.

'The villa lies in a hollow,' Eiluned explained. 'It's only a small place, not a real villa such as one might find near the Great North Road, but that is what my father preferred it to be called. I spent my childhood there, with Elspeth. When the Saxons threatened the Glein crossing, we deserted the villa. Forest lies between the estate and the Saxons by the sea, and around the house is a low, crumbling wall. My father grew too old to keep the place in good repair. His sons followed Artus. One died in a riding accident, the other still follows Artus the Bear on his campaigns.' Her eyes betrayed her sorrow. Practical, Paulus drew us back to the point.

'That sounds alright,' Paulus said. 'What d'you think?' He looked at me, but I only shrugged.

'I suggest we make a move as soon as possible,' Pedr said. 'I'd say tomorrow morning at the latest.'

'That doesn't give us much time,' Peneli said.

'Better be in a hurry than see him gelded and decapitated by Ceorl in front of the whole village.' He smiled in the way that warriors do at the thought of the carnage.

'Then it's settled,' I agreed, 'We leave on the morrow, before the cock crows if we are to steal away without Ceorl's knowing.' I looked round their faces. There were shrugs and nods of agreement all round. Having decided thus we stealthily set about our preparations late into the night.

During the night the Saxon awoke several times, but we could make no sense of what he said, apart from the fact that his name was Aonghus. This rather puzzled me because, as far as I knew, Aonghus was a Celtic name. The thought troubled me for the rest of the night and I seem to remember bad dreams for that night. I'm not sure though, because my slumber was to be infinitely more troubled later in that year.

CHAPTER TWO

The Villa

Pedr woke us all before sunrise. The morning air was cold and I was reluctant to leave my bed. When I did manage to get up and the tiredness flowed out of my limbs, I remembered the Saxon. He was still laying near the brazier, though this had now gone out. He was wrapped in furs from each of our beds which someone had taken the trouble to borrow during the night. Now I knew why I felt so cold.

'Think we ought to wake him?' Pedr asked me.

'Yes,' I answered. 'Unless you feel like carrying him again.' And so Pedr roused him. Eiluned stepped over to his side and helped him up.

'How do you feel?' she asked.

The man answered with another question: 'Where am I? my head . . .' Paulus stooped over the man. 'You're among friends. You ought to thank us.'

'You are my rescuers? Thank you.'

Pedr frowned. 'I'd rather he saved the thanks until later. Right now,' he turned to the man. 'I'd like to see you get on your feet.'

Shakily, we helped Aonghus to an upright position. 'I feel as though I have been asleep for years with a head filled with ale,' he remarked. He didn't strike me as one who could take much ale.

I looked at Peneli. 'Can he travel?'

'On horseback.'

'We have three mounts,' Paulus said. 'And one of those we'll need to carry baggage.'

'We are going on a journey?' Aonghus enquired. Eiluned released him and he stood uncertainly on his own feet.

'Not too far,' Elspeth said.

'Where am I now?'

'Ceorl's camp,' Pedr answered. 'We can't stay here; Ceorl hates every Saxon as an evil viper. That reminds me, we don't know anything about you yet.'

'My name is . . .'

'Save it,' Paulus said. 'We can discuss that later. The sun'll be up soon. I don't feel like explaining where we're

21

going to Ceorl. Leaving camp past Bledig will be a hard enough task.'

Paulus was right. Perhaps the loss of us would not mean much to Ceorl, but Ceorl followed Artus on his campaigns and Artus' army consisted largely of a cavalry force. Ceorl was not going to allow us to ride out with three horses when there were only fifteen in all in the camp.

We set about collecting our belongings together for the journey, while Paulus and Pedr went to fetch the horses.

We decided to carry as little as possible. Food, clothes and furs constituted most of what we did take with us. Otherwise, for myself, I took some valuable tools from my forge and my most treasured heirloom, my grandfather's sword which he had carried into battle whilst serving under Ambrosius Aurelianus.

The first golden haze touched the horizon as we mounted the horses; Aonghus and Peneli on one of the great black steeds, and Eiluned and Elspeth on the other. I laughed at Eiluned who was sitting almost across the horse's neck due to the great hulk of Elspeth behind her. Elspeth, although a woman, was the most well-built person among us.

Paulus undertook to lead the horses whilst Pedr and myself walked alongside. For the journey I wore my grandfather's sword, partly for convenience and partly for protection should the need arise. I knew how to use a sword, though I rarely did so.

At the gate, Bledig the guardian was asleep. We crept by him but he was awakened by the sound of the baggage horse. He started up only to be silenced by Pedr's blade resting at his throat. 'Ssshhhh,' Pedr hissed, and then put his hand hard over Bledig's mouth. He removed the blade from his throat and cracked Bledig on the back of the head with the pommel. Bledig fell silently to the earth.

We left by the rear entrance, and so we went down the track and then widely circled the rock so as to be unseen by the other sentries. The only sounds were the thud of horses' hooves and the creak of leather in the early dawn.

When we had fully circled the rock, the sunrise shone in our faces. The air seemed to lose some of its freshness. It was the middle of spring and the grip of winter which had persisted into yesterday seemed fully over.

We travelled fast until we reached the valley of the river which flowed down to Durobrivae. We didn't intend to enter the town itself, but to detour into the valley of a tributary. Eiluned showed us the way, consulting with her old friend Elspeth to reassure herself that she was guiding us the right way.

We halted for a time in the valley whilst Pedr and I cut down some branches from the ash trees to construct make-shift bows for hunting. We sharpened twigs for arrows. The bows were effective at close range. It was after we had finished shaping these crude weapons that we rested, and this gave us our first opportunity to question Aonghus. We moved swiftly during that morning, and Pedr and myself became separated from the others whilst we covered our tracks and watched for any sign of pursuit. We walked side by side in the valley, surveying the gently rolling landscape, searching in the shadowed areas of forest.

'Wet weather yesterday, and now the weather's fine. Not perfect conditions for covering our trail,' Pedr said, thrashing at some of the tall grass with his sword.

'We're doing alright,' I assured him. 'What's your opinion of the Saxon?'

'He's a good excuse to get out of Ceorl's camp. I felt like a change of scenery, besides I don't trust Ceorl a great deal. He was respected by the other people too much. Ceorl's as hard as a nail and just as easy to hammer.'

At this remark I laughed prodigiously, and then set about covering some of the tracks myself.

We rested in the shade of a willow on the banks of the river. The air was humid, though not greatly uncomfortable. The horses were sweating after driving them hard all morning and so we allowed them to occupy most of the shade afforded by the tree, while we sat on the grass. I was still curious as to how Aonghus, by all accounts a Saxon, came to have a Celtic name, and so I began the questioning with this.

'My father was Saxon, my mother a Celt of the Amporii tribe,' Aonghus said. 'I lived among Saxons. They were un-friendly to my mother because she was a Celt. During the winter, one of our hunting parties was lost. We found those who had not been taken prisoner by their attackers, their bodies mutilated and dangling from the trees of the forest. Many fathers and sons had been lost. It had been a carefully planned attack by the Celts, they had ventured far into our territory, killed half of a large hunting-party and taken the rest prisoner. My father was not among them. They blamed my mother for informing the Celts of our position. They said that she'd told them about the party. She couldn't tell what they were saying. She could not speak the language of the Saxons. I saw the look in her eyes when one of them ran her through. They held me and my father while they butchered her.'

'They let you go free?' Peneli asked.

'That was not their intention,' Aonghus replied. 'They took us out of the Saxon territory into Blackhorse country. They said they were leaving us to the Celts. They thought they were being merciful in so doing. "Giving us a chance". We had no weapons, and I have no use with anything larger than a knife anyway. We were stalked for two days and nights by Artus' border patrol. My father caught a spear in his entrails and died. I was hit on the head by a spear. They left me for dead. There were no weapons on my body for them to take. I wandered for days aimlessly. The wound in my head seemed to have healed. I hunted with a stick which I split at the end to make it sharp.'

'How did you come to be lying on the track up to Ceorl's camp?' Pedr enquired.

Aonghus grinned. 'Chasing a boar. There was a low branch on the track. I struck my head and knocked myself out. I woke up and tried to crawl along the track. The last thing I remember about that was feeling the blood flow around my ears. I suppose I fell unconscious again. I'd no idea there was a camp up the track or I'd never have ventured so near.'

'Artus' horsemen show little mercy,' Eiluned said.

'They have their duty to perform,' I answered her.

'That doesn't include cutting strangers down with no questions asked,' she argued. I could have taken up the argument against her, but I didn't, partly because of Aonghus and mostly because I didn't want to fall from her favour.

'If you're not a warrior, what were you to the Saxons?' Paulus wanted to know. I think he was under the popular impression that all Saxons were warlike barbarians.

'I am a carpenter,' Aonghus returned.

'And I a blacksmith,' I said. 'Together we can put the villa to rights in no time.'

We discussed the wars between the Saxons and the Celts

for some while, but when the sun had passed noon we rose stiffly from the ground and remounted the horses.

It was when the sun sank lower in the western sky that Pedr noticed a movement atop one of the hills which rose starkly to our left. We had kept close to the northern side of the river throughout the journey, and so if an enemy lurked in these hills we were not protected by the river.

Soon after Peder had first spotted the movement, I saw it too and by this time we had moved on a little. The thing or person was following us. We stuck close together for a time. We continued to spy the shape atop the hill at intervals, a dark silhouette, unknown and menacing, until we were overshadowed by a forested section of the hillside. Then we heard a sudden cry and far-off hoof beats. We looked to the trees which advanced down to meet the flood-plain of the river. Quite suddenly we were in among the trees. The hoofbeats paused, then resumed then paused again. Pedr, Paulus and I drew our swords. My grandfather's sword seemed too old to be formidable in anyone's hand, least of all mine, but it's weight brought comfort to my beating heart. We were silent, but we all asked the same question. Who were they? There was more than one rider, we could tell by the sound of the horses trampling through the bracken. The sounds now seemed to come closer now draw away again. Paulus handed the lead of the packhorse to Elspeth. We stopped moving. We could hear the sound of the birds, the breeze and whoever was following us. Then we saw him. It was Ceorl, and he had emerged alone from the bushes, his sword still in the scabbard, but his spear delicately poised. I didn't trust him, and guessed there must be many others of our old tribe hidden nearby. 'I'll take those horses,' he said, and when none of us moved five other horsemen emerged from the bushes in the forest to surround us. Walwyn was among their number.

Paulus moved to the horses as if to help the riders down. Suddenly his sword whipped up and struck the flank of Elspeth and Eiluned's horse. 'Go!' he shouted and the horse bolted. Aonghus dug his heels into the horse that carried him and Peneli. I saw Walwyn start as the charging steeds came towards him. He slipped and fell from his mount as the horse sidestepped the charge instinctively. Perhaps Walwyn did it on purpose to let Eiluned escape, perhaps not, we had no way of telling. It all happened so quickly. The next thing I knew, Pedr had mounted Walwyn's horse and was playing havoc around the circle of horsemen.

Walwyn had leapt to his feet and was threatening me with his spear, advancing slowly, teeth bared. It seemed strange that he who was once a friend was now my potential killer. He was careless with the weapon, using it too cautiously, as you would use a shield. I caught hold of the shaft and pushed it back into his belly. He stumbled and fell to be caught by the flying hooves of the horse which was dancing away from Pedr's onslaught. I whirled just in time to see Ceorl charging towards me with spear levelled. I managed to dodge behind a tree but the spearhead ripped my thigh. The next instant Ceorl was engaged in a tussle with Pedr, each violently trying to dismount the other. Paulus was struggling to hold off two horsemen with his sword. One of these was armed with a spear the other with a sword and shield. I tried to rush to his aid but collapsed, fainting at the pain in my thigh and the loss of blood. Pedr managed to overcome Ceorl and the man fell with a thud to the ground. Pedr then scattered Paulus' assailants who were half-heartedly attacking a former friend and pulled him up onto his horse. I managed to crawl to Ceorl's horse and to struggle onto its back unseen. Ceorl was on his feet again and was trying to drag me from the horse, but Pedr's ceaselessly swirling blade struck him on the back and he released his grip on my leg momentarily.

With a frantic dash we broke out of the circle of attackers and made swiftly off in the direction that the others had gone.

I heard Ceorl yelling and cursing at his men as the distance between us lengthened.

We rode fast to catch up with the rest of our companions. We met them where the trees thinned and the river was once more clearly in sight. I wrapped and bound tightly a piece of cloth around my wound and Peneli said she would search it for me when we made camp.

We made camp on the banks of the tributary river that night, we had reached the junction sooner than we had expected due to the speed of our flight. A large fire was lit, its crackling flames and twisting smoke to keep the wolves at bay and it was in this fire that Peneli heated the blade of her knife. My wound was not deep and to the bone and so the flesh was not likely to have more than a scar. Peneli did her work quickly and then bound up the wound in another piece of cloth. The pain subsided to a dull ache and I fell into a light sleep. Through the night scenes of the battle rushed into my head, and my legs twitched as I remembered the movement of the horses, the flashing blades. I had seen little fighting in the past, having refused to fight, and this light skirmish had made a deep impression. At last I fell into a deep sleep and the next thing I remember was Pedr waking me early the next morning. My leg was stiff and I walked with a limp. The days' ride took us up the river and out of its valley. We made our way onto the road from Durobrivae to Lindum. We had avoided Durobrivae because of the concentration of Blackhorse soldiers in the town. These were part of Artus' extensive border patrol. The road was a boundary almost, though one could travel a considerable way to the east of it without seeing any Saxons.

We crossed a bridge over a river and a short while later we came to another. This was the crossing of the little river Glien where Artus had struck his first victory against the Saxons in establishing a frontier. As we expected, there was a permanent camp on the other side of the bridge where several patrolmen were resting up for the night. We approached this by the light of a half-moon. I felt suddenly aware of the horse which carried me. Such mounts were valuable to Artus who had gone to great lengths to produce and train a sizeable stock of the great black steeds. They came from the North where they originated from an inter-breeding of Fell ponies and some Friesians which were stationed on the wall by the Romans.

We crossed the bridge slowly and one of the men stepped out into the road in front of us, his hands on his hips. He was a tall man and he wore no arms or armour. Blackhorse patrolmen on this bridge rarely expected any trouble. 'Greetings traveller,' the soldier said looking at me as I was in front of the rest. I nodded in response to his greeting. The question he asked was as I had expected; 'Those are mightily fine horses you travel on. From whence did you – er – acquire them?'

'We come from Ceorl's camp,' I replied, 'we're on our way to Lindum.'

'Ceorl's camp, eh? Can't say I've heard of it. What's your

business in Lindum? Must be pretty important if your Chieftain can spare those horses.'

I indicated Aonghus with my hand. 'We're escorting him to Lindum. He has some valuable information for Artus's authorities there.'

'Saxon?' The soldier craned his head around me to look at Aonghus.

I nodded.

'Why didn't you hand him over in Durobrivae? The men there could have made sure he'd got to Lindum.'

I forced a false grin. 'There's the – er – question of a reward.'

The soldier laughed. 'You tribesmen are all the same,' he remarked.

'Why do you travel with women?'

'We met the big one and her friend back down the road. Their horse had gone lame so we gave them the Saxon's.' The lie seemed unconvincing to me.

'What about the other?' The soldier was looking at Peneli.

I thought of an amusing terminological inexactitude. 'She,' I grinned. 'Is the Saxon's reward from Ceorl.'

Again the soldier laughed. I laughed with him and Pedr and Paulus sniggered, though Peneli looked disgusted.

I looked over to the camp. The soldiers were gathered around a fire. There were three of them, one lying on his back reciting to his comrades of the supernaturally good-looking girl he had met in Glevum last year. 'Mind if we share your fire tonight, soldier? We are weary, especially the women.'

The soldier turned to the others. They had heard my request. They replied to the other man's glance with shrugs and similar 'alright-by-me' gestures. The soldier turned to me again. 'Alright. But don't let that Saxon near me when I'm wrapped in my blanket. I'll be sleeping with one eye open.' And with that he returned to his former position near the fire.

I dismounted as did the others. I looked at them and blew out a heavy sigh of relief. They all smiled, except Peneli.

We put our horses with the soldiers' with their reins secured to an elongated log raised on two posts.

As requested, Aonghus made his bed a short distance away from the soldiers. The rest of us gathered around the fire with the exception of Eiluned who went over to keep Aonghus company before retiring.

The soldier who had questioned us said: 'What is your name, tribesman?'

'Ailin Rhydwyn. What is yours, soldier?'

'Ystffan Irfon. My companions are Meilyr, Heddwyn and Eirig.' The three men nodded.

'My friends are Pedr and Paulus.' I indicated them. 'The women are Peneli and Elspeth. The one talking to the Saxon is Eiluned.'

I questioned him about the strength of his force and their business but he was reluctant to tell me much of his plans. At last he turned away and joined his companions and we all slept peacefully, feeling that we could trust one another, despite these troubled times.

Again we started early the following morning. The sun had only just risen as we set off down the road shouting cheery goodbyes to the soldiers. We had no intention of going to Lindum. Eiluned guided us from the road to the East and we travelled for the following day in a North-Easterly direction. We felt in good spirits and sang for most of the journey, the women's clear voices joining our own, and sometimes singing alone. This made the hours pass quickly till we should arrive at our new home. There were many tracks and various landmarks to follow, but at last we rode down into a hollow on one side of which the forest encroached, and situated in its bottom a modest Roman-style house and outbuildings surrounded by a low wall.

We approached the villa by way of an overgrown track down the side of the hollow which twisted and turned until it grew somewhat wider and passed through the gate-less gateway. We dismounted in the cobbled courtyard. There were stables and the blacksmith's shop on either side and the squat house in front. There was a dilapidated well in the centre of the yard.

Eiluned was the first to venture towards the house. For myself I walked over and inspected the blacksmith's shop taking note of which tools still remained and the condition the forge was in. After this inspection I followed the others into the house.

Unlike the rather more extravagant houses I had seen,

the villa had only one floor and a low roof. The atrium, or so Eiluned called it, was the largest and most decorated room. The walls were painted with scenes from one of the Romans' Gods' lives and the floor was largely mosaic. There were two doors at the back of the room leading to the kitchen on the left and the bedrooms and a small study on the right. Eiluned paused in the study. There was a seatless cross-legged chair overturned in the centre of the room. She righted it and felt its contours. I guessed that the chair had once belonged to her father.

I left Eiluned alone and returned to the atrium. She followed me shortly afterwards and went to the shrine in the corner of the room. There were such shrines in all Roman houses for the burning of incense to the ancestral gods of the house. Eiluned stood looking into the mosaics on the shrine, and then she left the atrium and went outside. She returned soon afterwards with a small wooden cross she had brought with her. It was a crude affair, held together with sinew, just a couple of grey twigs. She stood this on the shrine. I knew the symbol, the symbol of the Christians who worshipped the one God and the man who died on the cross. It perturbed me to see this god's cross standing in the shrine. I moved closer to her. 'No. Do not worship your god here. It will displease the ancestors and bring misfortune upon this house.'

She picked up the cross. 'Very well, I will worship my God elsewhere. You needn't fear the ancestors of this house. They would not harm us.'

'I still bear respect for the old ways. This new religion is faith enough for women.'

She smiled gently and I knew that it pained her that I did not wish to hear her tales of the new Lord, the Messiah, and his teachings. I had no use for this God, I knew only the practical things about life, and my gods were enough for me.

'Who is it you worship, Ailin?'

'Mithras.'

'The god of the soldiers.' She sighed. The others came into the atrium after exploring the house.

'There are three bedrooms,' Pedr said. 'The women can share one room.'

'I'll unload the packhorse,' said Paulus and he left the atrium. I followed to help him.

It was getting dark outside. We began to untie the ropes holding our baggage onto the horse. 'What do you think?' I asked.

'Not a bad place,' Paulus answered. 'We could make something of it with a bit of hard work.'

'I think we could. I'll start tomorrow and repair the forge.' The baggage came loose and we carried it into the house discussing on the way the various repairs that had to be carried out and the many materials that we had to discover to do them. We set it down on that intricately-patterned floor of the atrium and we all sorted out what belonged to each person. I carried my furs into one of the bedrooms and slung them down on the bare wooden frame. I put my tools in the blacksmith's shop and then went back to the atrium where we lit a fire on top of some rocks and ate a meal. Paulus and Pedr decided to go hunting in the forest the next morning. I intended to remain wrapped in my furs until noon after the days of waking early. Even back at the camp our time was not our own. Ceorl liked us up early for work.

I did not go straight away to sleep that night. I lay awake and thought about the journey, about Ceorl's camp and the Saxons. I pondered on Aonghus's story and, when dreams were about to overtake conscious thought I wondered about Eiluned. Now she was free from Walwyn, would she return my affection? There seemed a chance she would bend her favour to me. I rolled over and bade Pedr goodnight. He was already asleep. I realised then how little I now felt for Peneli. The thought of Eiluned warmed me inside and caused me to smile suddenly and childishly to myself. 'You can keep your witch, my friend,' I whispered in Pedr's direction and then I must have fallen asleep.

CHAPTER THREE

Merriam

We first saw Merriam in Lindum. After six days at the villa, Paulus, Eiluned and I had undertook a journey to the market at Lindum to pick up some supplies. I needed certain things to repair my forge to bring it back into full working order and therefore make it of some use to the household. Lindum must have been the largest settlement I had ever seen, and the great number of people who filled the streets was almost frightening. They seemed perfectly at home and bustled hither and thither, calling out to one another, making coarse jokes, and commenting rudely on the goods displayed before them. Paulus and I joined in and found that we could saunter along quite happily, looking for the things we wanted to buy. But supplies were forgotten by Paulus and I when we set eyes on Merriam. She was the daughter of a chieftain who had his lands not far away from Ceorl's. And it was to Ceorl that she was betrothed, though Ceorl I think preferred to take his pleasures outside the bond of marriage.

Eiluned had vanished into the throng of the market place and Paulus and I stood and simply gazed at the girl as she wandered around the Forum. She seemed at her ease here, greeting friends as they passed arguing with the stall-vendors through her maid, and many admiring glances went her way. She was tall and shapely and dressed in the finest cloth that Celtic craftsmen could offer. Her hair was long and straight and shone the colour of bronze flowing down her back.

'They say she is the mistress of many warriors,' Paulus remarked.

'Of that I'm not surprised. Look at her Paulus! Do you not envy the good fortune of Ceorl?'

'By the gods yes! What are we standing here for? Let's go over and greet her.'

Paulus began to walk towards her. I called after him: 'Paulus! Are you mad?' but he ignored me.

Paulus began chatting to Merriam's maidservant and she accepted his offer to carry her mistress's purchases around the Forum. Merriam turned to Paulus. 'I thank you sir for relieving my maidservant of her burden. What is your name?'

'My name is Paulus. My friend is Ailin Rhydwyn.'

Merriam looked at me. 'I have heard of you, Ailin. I am Merriam, betrothed to Ceorl.'

'Poor girl,' the maidservant remarked quietly.

'Do I know you?' I asked, though I couldn't imagine how I could have forgotten any communication with this beauty.

'I am Ceorl's woman,' she answered. 'You are the warrior who will not take up his sword.'

'I am a blacksmith,' I corrected her.

'All Celts are warriors,' said she. 'Why is it you do not take up sword against the Saxons?'

I shrugged. It was answer enough. She soon forgot her question, turning back to Paulus. 'Are you a warrior, little friend?'

Paulus seemed unhurt by her remark about his size. 'You could say that, though as you see I am of little use in a hard fight.'

'I am sure that your valour matches that of Ceorl himself.'

'And that says very little for you,' the maidservant put in an aside. I could tell by her impudence that the maidservant was also a close friend of Merriam.

'I understand that it is an honour to capture the heart of Ceorl,' I said to balance the maidservant's remark.

'An honour? I should be "honoured"?' Merriam seemed surprised.

'It is not Ceorl's heart she has captured. He has none. Ceorl is a fool with the mind of a child,' said the maidservant pertly. It was refreshing to hear the man's name in open dispute among women.

'You are unkind, Bronwen,' Merriam returned.

We walked on through the market crowd. I caught sight of Eiluned. She was weighed down by the bundle of goods she carried. I compared her outwardly with Merriam. She seemed spindly beside this hot-blooded wench of Ceorl's. And yet I knew I felt something rather more than a physical attraction for Eiluned. I called to her and she came towards me. I took the bundle from her. 'Whose purchases are those Paulus carries? Surely he is not given to buying ladies finery.'

'Paulus has found his head turned by one Merriam,' I answered.

'Merriam? Not Ceorl's betrothed?' she breathed in surprise.

'The same.'

'The idiot! Does he want to bring Ceorl down around our ears?'

I sighed and smiled. 'It's time we started back. How do we drag him away?'

'I'll leave that to you,' Eiluned said. I handed her the bundle back and walked over to Merriam.

'Can you spare my friend's company?' I asked good-humouredly. 'We must now return.'

'So soon?' Merriam said. 'We should have met earlier. How far is it from Lindum to Ceorl's camp?'

'We aren't going to Ceorl's camp,' Paulus said.

I frowned at him. 'And I'm afraid Paulus can't tell you where we are actually going for reasons of health.'

'Meaning?' Paulus said angrily.

'Meaning shut up or I'll shut you up,' I explained. I looked at Merriam and smiled. 'Ceorl will no doubt explain all when you see him. We – er – had a disagreement with him.'

Merriam laughed. Paulus handed the goods back to the maidservant and we bade them farewell.

We walked back to Eiluned in good spirits. Eiluned made a short joke out of Paulus's new desire and then we left the forum. We loaded the goods onto the packhorse and were soon on our way out of the town and down the road.

If we followed the road, which was certainly the safest way in view of our situation on the border country, the ride would take two days. We decided not to waste time in getting back and Eiluned guided us away from the road and onto the ancient pathways she knew so well. Soon we lost sight of the road and travelled at as near a gallop as we could muster from the horse, over the fields.

We made camp that night in the open, our shelter some trees. We were only about half a day's ride from the villa now according to Eiluned and we felt satisfied with our progress and the goods we had obtained from the market.

After filling my belly, I felt nothing like sleep and so I wandered around a short distance from the camp and occupied my mind with plans of what I could manufacture once the forge was repaired. Of course I would need iron, but the ore was quarried in the hills to the west only a day's ride from the villa. I made a note in my mind to make a journey there when I could accumulate some wealth from hunting to bargain with. Iron was not cheap with the continuing Saxon wars. It was mainly used for the making of arms for Artus's men and for the Northern kingdoms. Swords and spearheads were the things Ceorl wanted most from his 'smiths.

My chain of thought was suddenly broken by the sound of footsteps behind. I turned. It was Paulus. 'Can't you sleep either?' I asked.

'I've got things on my mind,' he said.

'Like Merriam, for instance?' I enquired.

'Perhaps,' he replied, then asked; 'Ailin, d'you think if she regards me favourably I stand any chance?'

'You could have a damn good time one night if she does, provided Ceorl doesn't get to know.'

He looked sullen. 'I wish – it isn't only one night I seek.'

'By Mithras Paulus! You've only ever spoken to the girl once.'

'I knew her when I was a child,' he argued.

'Then you should have taken your opportunity then.'

'She would never have looked at me twice then. It's my size! I'm cursed by the gods for becoming a Christian.'

At this I laughed. 'In the bed of a wench we are all the same size. Don't worry about it, Paulus. Look at me. Some say I'm too tall.'

Paulus nodded. 'Perhaps I should send her a gift.'

'Such as?'

'Oh, I don't know. Maybe it's not such a good idea.'

'No, don't alter your mind. You'll find something. Right now, I grow weary. Are you turning in?'

'No,' Paulus said. 'I think I'll stay here a while.'

'Alright. Try not to awaken me when you decide to come back to camp. Goodnight.' And with that I walked slowly back to the cluster of trees where our campfire burned orange.

Eiluned was not asleep. She sat up, wrapped in her furs. 'Paulus is lovesick tonight,' I said, crouching beside her.

Eiluned laughed. 'I wonder how they're doing back at the villa,' she said.

'They should be safe with Pedr to look after them,' I assured her.

Again she was amused. 'But is Pedr alright with Peneli to look after him?' She chuckled.

I didn't reply. My thoughts had suddenly become confusedly caught up with her. I wanted to take her there and then; I wanted to convey to her my emotions, but there seemed only one way to do so. Yet I didn't want to make love to her. It seemed too barbaric tonight. What I felt was so much more than friendship. She seemed to see my thoughts through my eyes, and she quickly turned away and lay down to sleep. 'Goodnight Eiluned,' I said.

'Goodnight,' she responded and closed her eyes in sleep, or perhaps to cut me off from her.

I scrambled over to my furs and covered myself, reclining on my back. After some time I fell asleep.

I woke up in the middle of the night. The fire was burnt low. Eiluned was asleep, but the familiar form of Paulus wrapped in his furs was not there. I shook myself to clear the fog of sleep from my mind and sat up. I looked around. Paulus was nowhere to be seen. I looked over to my right and saw that his horse was gone. I threw off my fur and pulled the cloak that I was lying on around my shoulders. I stood up and walked over to where Eiluned lay. I bent down and gently shook her. She woke up.

'What is it?' she asked rubbing her eyes.

'Paulus is missing. His horse has gone too.'

Eiluned sat up and surveyed the camp. 'His rugs are still here. He must be back later.'

We built up the fire and waited. Just before sunrise we heard steady hoofbeats. We ran out of the trees. Paulus was coming towards us. His horse was sweating and panting, its body cut and bleeding in several places. Paulus himself was in a worse condition. His clothes were blood-stained and his face cut and bruised. Sweat was pouring from him. He held loosely in his hand a long, broad blade. The sword was enormous. He smiled when he saw us and then tumbled from his horse. He raised his head once and then it dropped and he lay motionless. The wind swept over him.

Eiluned and I ran to where he lay on the dew-laden grass. I knelt down beside him and rolled him over. I listened for his heartbeat. It was pounding, his chest heaved. 'He's alive,' I said with relief in my voice.

'Thank God,' said Eiluned.

I loosed his clothing and looked for any other wounds apart from those on his face. There was a deep cut in his side. Blood oozed from it and stained his leather jerkin and matted his furs. 'It's bad,' I reported.

'We must staunch the flow or his life will go from him,' Eiluned said urgently.

We carried Paulus to the camp and set him down on his furs. While Eiluned removed Paulus's furs and jerkin, I put more wood on the fire and re-kindled it. I then fetched Paulus's own sword and thrust it into the fire. I waited for the blade to turn bright red .'I'll hold him down,' I said. 'Can you do the rest?'

'I've seen Peneli do it often enough,' she replied confidently.

The blade took a while to heat. When finally the red glow came, I drew it from the fire and felt the heat against my face. I nodded to Eiluned who came over and took the sword from me. I walked over to Paulus and held him by the shoulders. Nervously, Eiluned brought the blade closer to the wound. She touched the finger-length cut with the tip of the blade. The flowing blood boiled and Paulus screamed out as she knelt down and placed the flat of the blade across the wound. There was the vile aroma of burning flesh. The skin around the wound turned black as it burned. Paulus struggled and then passed out with the pain. I released his shoulders and wiped away the sweat that stood out on my brow.

'Where do you suppose he received a wound like that?' Eiluned asked.

'This is disputed country. If it belongs to anyone the Saxons have the stronger claim to this land nowadays. Paulus must have met up with a band of Saxon warriors.'

'But why did he leave the camp in the first place, I wonder?'

The thought was puzzling. I scratched my head. 'He was in a fever after today, I think. He probably went for a ride to cool his blood and strayed too far east. Perhaps we wandered too far from the road. We'd better move on.'

We packed our gear and set off on our way home. I constructed a horse-litter from some branches and furs for

Paulus. Just before we left, he woke up for a short time and reminded me about the great sword he had brought back with him. I fetched it from where he had fallen from his horse and gave it to him. He nursed it as though it were a child and fell asleep again.

We paused before noon and Eiluned attended to the injured horse Paulus had ridden on his mysterious journey.

It was mid-afternoon when at last we reached the villa. Pedr helped me carry the litter with Paulus on it down the slope of the hollow to the house. Everybody wanted to know how Paulus came to be in his present condition, and since neither I or Eiluned knew, we all had to wait for Paulus to wake up and could barely keep our patience.

One thing I did know was that the sword Paulus had returned with was Saxon in its origin.

Paulus woke after sundown that night. We helped him to his place at the long dining table which Aonghus had constructed along with the benches we sat on. We feasted on the rewards of a recent hunting excursion by Pedr and then turned all our attention to Paulus.

'We're waiting for an explanation, Paulus,' said Peneli.

An explanation was not forthcoming however hard we tried to persuade him to tell us what he had been doing and where. We were exasperated, and started calling him names, but he kept his stubborn silence, and in the end we gave up. Shortly after he'd eaten, Paulus went to his bedroom. We had to remain ignorant.

Before turning in myself, I went to his room and found him awake. Aonghus was not there as he was adding the finishing touches to a piece of furniture in the atrium.

'Well?' I said.

'You want to know what happened,' Paulus said. It was not a question.

'Yes.' I answered, expecting him to tell me to leave him alone. But he did not. I think he felt like getting his troubles off his chest.

'I went to get the sword,' Paulus explained. I didn't understand.

'The sword? Why ever did you want the sword of a Saxon?'

Paulus sighed. 'As a gift. For Merriam. It was what I

said – about needing a gift for her, and what she said about my valour too.'

The whole thing seemed stupid. 'You maniac! You nearly got yourself killed to win a trophy for a woman? Paulus, I come to doubt your sanity.'

'You said I stood a chance with her. Do you now deny that? Should I bother to send her the gift?'

'I don't deny you could win the affections of this woman, you self-conscious idiot. And if you don't send her the gift after nearly killing yourself achieving it you'd be completely out of your mind. Tell me, how did you get hold of the sword exactly?'

Again Paulus sighed. Then he began his story: 'I thought of the idea after you left me. The Blackhorsemen on the road told me the Saxons were becoming bolder nowadays when they heard tell of Artus's troubles at home, with his unfaithful wife. Twice they said they'd encountered them only a day's canter east of the road in the past winter. Only small raiding parties, mind you, but enough to give the soldiers cause for concern . . .'

'They told you this the night we camped at the Glien crossing?'

'That's right. Anyway, we were well east of the road last night, so I thought that if I looked a little further east and hard enough, I was bound to come across some Saxons sometime.'

'You went LOOKING for trouble?' I was astounded. I sat down on the side of his bed. 'Go on.'

'Well, I found some of the bastards alright. They were camped on the banks of some stream or other. A hunting party, I think. There were many hunting spears lying carelessly about,' he paused for me to take the scene in. 'There were a lot of trees and bushes about. I got down from my horse and tied it a short distance away in a thick clump of trees. I crept through the undergrowth and looked around. There was only one guard wandering around and he seemed half-asleep,' (I thought of a Saxon with Bledig's face.) 'The others were snoring away merrily. I think they'd been drinking. Then I saw the leader, I think he was the leader, with this monstrous sword lying next him. I sneaked round and carefully stole it. I had the thing in my hands! I made my way back around their camp and I was nearly to my horse when the guard spotted me. He wasn't sure at first and he levelled his spear and came closer. I caught hold of the spear. I took him by surprise and knocked him over. He shouted to his friends just before the sword I'd stolen went through his belly. They came rushing at me but I had already untied my horse and scrambled on his back. They tried to grab my legs but I just went mad like I do when I fight and I got the horse moving. Then one of them got close enough to take a jab with his sword and that's how I got the wound. He got his leader's sword in the mouth. But there were a lot of 'em and I would have been overwhelmed but for my horse. Good old Cadfan! They tried to injure him and he lost his temper. He reared up and scared the daylights out of them. Saxons fear horses. One of their gods is a horse! They ran back and I got Cadfan under control and made him gallop like mad. They caught me a couple of times with their spears around the head. But I escaped.' He seemed proud of his exploits, and pointed out that he had achieved his purpose.

'Only just,' I said. 'You were very foolish.'

'Will *you* give the sword to her? I can't get her out of my mind Ailin. I must do this, for honour's sake, and I don't care if her man *is* Ceorl she must know the way I feel.'

'Why don't you deliver it?'

'Partly because my wound tires me and partly because, well, I'm not that good with women and words of flattery.'

At this I laughed. 'You idiot! You wander into a hornets' nest of Saxons and now you're afraid to face a woman.'

'Take the sword for me,' he persisted. 'Tell her it's from a – er – valorous friend.'

'Very poetic,' I sniggered. 'Very well, I'll take her the sword the day after tomorrow when I go to bargain for some iron-ore.'

'Thanks,' he said. I left the room as Aonghus entered.

I could understand now why Paulus didn't want to disclose the purpose of his trip at the dinner table. Peneli would have been in fits of laughter. She'd laugh to disguise her jealousy. Pedr, though in a way betrothed to her, cared very little for her. Everyone knew that, the joke was popular. Everyone knew except poor Peneli. I felt somehow sorry for her, but she had a habit of spoiling people's feelings for her, souring their good intentions with her coarse manner.

Pedr was beneath his furs when I retired to our bedroom.

I stripped off my outer clothes and got between my own coverings. 'How's Paulus?' Pedr enquired, his voice muffled by his furs.

I turned my head towards him and looked at the unruly mop of dark hair. 'He's picking up,' I replied.

'Good,' said Pedr and got further down in his covers.

CHAPTER FOUR

The Seeds of Discord

I spent the next morning repairing the forge. It was a sunny day with no air stirring, and during the afternoon I became very uncomfortable whilst using the forge to repair some old tools belonging to the villa.

Paulus was able to sit outside as the weather was good and he lent some assistance to Aonghus in constructing some more furniture for the old study.

Eiluned was caring for the wounded horse, that Paulus had named Cadfan, and Elspeth helped her to do so. I could see into the stable from my workshop which was opposite across the courtyard.

Late that afternoon, as the sun's rays were slanting arcoss the weeds in the yard, Aonghus finished his work and wandered into the stable to talk to Eiluned and Elspeth. Eiluned and her friend had watched over Cadfan all day long as the horse was in a bad way but too useful to lose. The wounds had worsened during the journey home as we had been too busy with Paulus to attend to the horse immediately and allow the cuts to heal over.

From where I worked I could hear the three of them laughing together, and it sent a strange chill through me. Aonghus was obviously amusing company. Somehow this angered me. I realised I was jealous, and how fond I was of Eiluned. I watched them conversing and burnt the metal of one of the tools after becoming too engrossed in observing them. After that I tried to ignore them and worked at my forge furiously despite the heat of the day.

When the sun was low in the Western sky, Pedr and I left Aonghus showing the women and Paulus how to carve small animals from wood and went up the western slope of the hollow to scout the terrain. Not far from the rim of the hollow flowed a stream in which we had decided to bathe.

Whilst bathing I noticed that the wound in my thigh was almost healed. I thanked the gods that I had not been crippled.

*

The following morning I collected the sword from Paulus's room and set off to the west heading for the camp of Dyfan, father of Merriam.

I had reached the camp by nightfall. It commanded a hill which rose above the other hills which surrounded it. I made my way steadily up the winding track to the main gate. There I was met by two guards who had watched my slow arrival. They were reluctant to let me enter at first, but I explained to them the reason for my visit and was permitted to enter. I heard them snigger as I passed through the gate. I didn't know why then, but I was soon to find out.

Merriam came from her father's longhut and greeted me. But she seemed distracted, and after handing over the gift from Paulus she bade me leave immediately. I walked to my horse and remounted and began to move slowly towards the gate. Then I heard a familiar voice from behind me and my heart leaped into my throat. 'Ailin Rhydwyn!'

I halted and after a pause I turned the horse around. I faced Ceorl. There seemed very little to say.

'Well, well,' Ceorl said. It seemed that Ceorl was unsuited to the phrase. He talked very little usually. He stood outside the door of the longhut. A crowd of tribesmen gathered around him from the cluster of huts in the background. The guards on the fences turned their attention from the landscape to me. I swallowed nervously, in that hostile ring.

'Get off the horse,' Ceorl ordered in his blunt manner. I obeyed. Ceorl walked to me and hit me hard in the jaw. I staggered backwards. I thought of striking back. There were too many others around. I decided to wait and see.

'Who sent the sword?' Ceorl demanded.

'I can't tell you,' I answered. What if he tortures it out of me? I thought, what will he do to Paulus if he finds out? Is it that important to him, or does he just wish to make a fool of me? Ceorl struck me again. I fell over but was soon on my feet again. The crowd jeered and I felt humiliated. 'Give 'im the lash, Ceorl!' a woman bawled. I wished that I'd brought grandfather's sword along. I could've run him through then and to hell with the consequences.

'Tell me,' Ceorl said.

'I'm not at liberty to do – ' Again I was sprawling in the dirt. I'd fallen on my belly. I blew the muck from my mouth and turned my head to look at him. 'No!' I yelled.

Ceorl's stern glare relaxed. He laughed. Laughed again so that it stirred the camp. They all started laughing, though none were sure exactly what was so funny. 'Why do I bother?' Ceorl asked himself aloud. I stood up. 'Get out of this camp,' he said. 'Go! Take the horse with you! Go before the scars that your friend gave me on my arse smart to remind me what I owe you. Tell whoever it was who sent you with this gift to come and face me himself. I've no time for you, blacksmith.' He spat contemptuously on the ground by my feet.

I wasn't sure what to do. I stood and looked at him for fifty heartbeats, then I turned away and got onto my horse. I thanked Mithras for allowing me to keep the animal. Ceorl called after me. I stopped and turned my head to face him. 'Tell your "valorous" friend that the duel also decides the fate of the horses you stole. Is your friend a man of his word?'

I nodded. I had no intention of letting Paulus go, but then his honour was at stake. I rode out of the encampment.

'I will be waiting!' Ceorl called as I galloped away down the winding track.

I rode to the iron ore quarry and there I exchanged some furs and valuables for a quantity of ready smelted iron. I had expected to have to take the ore and smelt it myself, but the man in charge of the quarry was generous. As a form of repayment for this generosity I stayed the night there and spent the next morning forging swords alongside his own blacksmiths.

I arrived back at the villa at noon the following day. I was met by Paulus, whom I was glad to see was on his feet again in the courtyard. 'Did you deliver my trophy?' he wanted to know.

I had time to say 'Yes' just as the others gathered around me. I showed them the iron and the response to the nature of the stuff was favourable. I took it into the workshop and set it down near the forge. There wasn't a great amount of iron, but enough to make a few small repairs to various odds and ends around the villa.

I spent the afternoon helping Pedr lay a few stones on the wall around the house which was crumbling in places, as

Eiluned had anticipated. All the while I was doing this work I was thinking about Paulus and Merriam and Ceorl.

After supper, I went for a walk around the hollow. Paulus followed me. We stood on the forest side looking up at the stars.

'Well?' he said.

'Well what?' I asked, full well knowing what he meant. I was trying to avoid talking about it.

'What did she say to you?' Paulus wanted to know.

'Thank you,' I answered.

'You're lying, Ailin. What's wrong?'

I sighed heavily and transferred my gaze from the sky to the ground. 'Ceorl was there,' I said. I cursed myself for telling him, but he had a right to know.

'Where does he want to meet me?' Paulus asked.

'I didn't tell him who sent the sword,' I said.

'But he let you go. Does he want a duel with the sender?'

'Yes. But that doesn't mean . . .'

'. . . I'll go tomorrow. Where is he now? Dyfan's camp?'

We argued for a long time. He won. He finally got the whole story out of me. 'I'm not worried,' he concluded. 'I've clashed with Ceorl before. He would never fight me. We have a sort of friendship.'

'I hope you're right. A lot depends on it. If he does get nasty, as I think he will, you run like hell. We can do without the horses.'

Afterwards, we walked slowly back to the villa. In the atrium, they all sat around a brazier and talked. The last two days had been rather cold and misty and so a fire had been lit at night.

The talk was pleasant and amusing. I realised that I'd have to tell them about Ceorl. They'd want to know why I wanted the horses the next day. And so Paulus and I told the others the full story. There wasn't much response, only Pedr remarked jokingly that he 'should've known better'. The women were curious about the ins and outs of the story but there was very little comment. The pleasant talk stopped also, and we all went to bed except Eiluned and Aonghus. I could hear talking long into the night. I think he must have kissed her, perhaps more . . . I went to sleep with tears in my eyes.

*

It was dusk when Paulus and I led the horses in Dyfan's camp. We were met by the crowds who looked at Paulus with intense curiosity. The hag who had shouted for Ceorl to give me the lash on my previous visit came to Paulus's horse and touched him. 'You are the one?' Paulus nodded. The hag shook her head. 'Then go while you still have the chance, little warrior.' And Paulus did not move.

The crowd around us moved away to the side when Ceorl appeared in front of us with old Dyfan at his side. Merriam was nowhere to be seen. 'Prepare to meet your end,' Paulus said, with humour in his voice. My nerves were on edge.

Ceorl laughed. I thanked my gods. It was a laugh of amusement, not a roar of triumph. 'Paulus Penwyn. YOU sent the sword? Ha! What competition! I stand no chance with the lady Merriam with such a handsome fellow as you seeking her affections, eh Dyfan?' The old chief grinned. 'Would you have us prepare food for your guests?'

We dined in Dyfan's longhut. There was plenty of food and a distinct lack of the Roman table manners we had at the villa, but we were hungry and in no mood for delicacy. When we had gorged ourselves and had our fill of Dyfan's ale, we talked. The talk at this table differed from that at our own. These men were true warriors. The talk was mainly concerned with the recent clashes with the Saxons, and more interesting to me, the talk concerning Artus. 'Who is this man to lead us,' Ceorl was saying, 'Who cannot control his own wife?'

'They say that she was condemned,' one of the tribesmen said, 'And the Prince of Belne rescued her from the flames.'

'It is sad that Wlanca has broken with Artus over a mere woman,' Dyfan put in, the grease from his meal running down his beard.

'Where is Winifred now?' Paulus asked.

'In Armorica with Wlanca, I've heard tell,' answered the tribesman who told us about Winifred's rescue by Wlanca.

'And while Artus chases around after a woman the fellowship he commands is divided and that weasel Mordrawt grows increasingly powerful in the North,' Dyfan scowled.

'What are the Saxons doing with all this going on?' I enquired.

'Who knows?' Dyfan replied. 'Some say that the Saxons will follow Mordrawt.'

'Is that not a good thing?' I wanted to know. 'Perhaps Mordrawt can bring Saxon and Briton together against a common enemy. We might see a lasting peace without feuding.'

'Artus has given us peace for a generation of men. I was there when he led the slaughter of the Saxon sons-of-bitches at Badon hill. If Artus falls, Britain is lost to the Saxons and the mad raiders from across the sea. When they have killed Artus they will turn against Mordrawt, they'll eat the guts of the land once they've stripped the flesh.'

'Will you follow Artus, then, if he leads an army against Mordrawt?' Paulus ventured.

'I shall be there,' Dyfan replied. He looked at Ceorl.

'I shall not,' Ceorl said. Dyfan scowled, but did not argue, perhaps for his daughter's sake. Merriam was not present at the feast.

I woke the next morning still sprawled across Dyfan's table. My head ached as if it had been split down the middle with an axe. I looked around for Paulus. He was on the floor next to me. I vomited and staggered up from the hard bench. Dyfan had gone to his bed, and doubtless Ceorl had tried to breach Merriam's. I kicked Paulus on the leg to wake him up. I wanted to get going. He moaned and complained that I had awoken him from a good dream, but we eventually got outside.

The morning air was fresh on this hilltop. It felt good after the stink of the longhut's hall. We walked to where we had left the horses. A guard watched over them. 'Ceorl says you are to take only three,' he informed us. We shrugged, neither of us in a mood to argue. We departed with three horses only.

After a days' ride, we were home again. Pedr was the first to greet us. He met us at the gate. He looked at the three horses. 'What's this, was the duel a draw?' he mused.

'We compromised,' I said. Eiluned, Peneli and Elspeth came running to us.

'Who won?' Elspeth asked.

'I sorted him out,' said Paulus.

'Then why are there only three horses now?' Eiluned asked. Everyone chuckled.

We stabled the horses and went inside. Aonghus was still hard at work, on some other piece of furniture for the villa. He had a habit of working hard, I think he meant it as some kind of repayment for our defiance in saving his life as we did. I didn't tell him but I would have found some other excuse to get away from Ceorl's camp anyway if we never came across Aonghus.

The women prepared a meal and we ate. I had not eaten all day after the feast at Dyfan's camp the previous night. As I ate now I remembered the grease running through Dyfan's beard and those of his warriors too, and that reminded me that I had to shave off my whiskers. All of us were clean shaven, though now Pedr was contemplating growing a handsome Celtic beard.

The next morning Paulus, Aonghus and I subjected ourselves to the agony of scraping away the growth of many days. Pedr gloated over our sore chins and fondly rubbed the bristles on his face to test their progress.

The day passed smoothly without incident as did the following days to the second passing of the full moon since our arrival at the villa.

CHAPTER FIVE

'Till the Burning of the Summer Fires, my Love

We settled back to enjoy the fruits of freedom in our new home, with the relief of knowing that Ceorl was no longer seeking after us. We made improvements to the villa. Aonghus and I repaired the woodwork, the fences and the wall. Pedr gathered certain plants with Peneli's help and restored the paintwork on the walls and the mosaics on the floor of the atrium and the study, wherever possible with our scanty supplies.

These were the best days of my life. I frequently went out riding on what had once been the estate of the villa with my friends, including the women, especially Eiluned. Though she seemed now to be Aonghus's woman, I still could not deny my feelings for her. Our, or rather my, relationship with her was completely innocent. I never kissed her nor held her close, as I would have liked. But such things do not last.

It was ten days to the midsummer festival when Pedr and I were at a loose end, and so we decided to pay a visit to the outlying land on horseback as we frequently did. During the whole time, Pedr seemed to be more alive than he had been for ages. I was glad of it. Pedr had been so aloof with regard to me since Peneli had turned her attentions from me to him, but today was different. I discovered the reason as we were making our way slowly home from the treck. 'Are you looking forward to your wedding?' I asked. Peneli was hinting a lot about midsummer weddings. It seemed as though the marriage was quite certain, to all but Pedr that is.

'I don't wish to marry anybody,' Pedr answered, the light of enjoyment in his eyes fading.

'I think Peneli has different ideas, old friend,' I told him.

'That's not my fault,' Pedr retorted as we rode around the rim of the hollow in which the villa lay. 'I think I must open her eyes soon.'

'She's not a woman to take rejection lightly,' I warned him.

'That's up to her,' he said and then we raced each other down to the villa.

I'm not sure how or when Pedr told Peneli that he did not wish to marry her. Afterwards Pedr avoided her though she seemed not to care. Only her eyes betrayed her feelings. They were misty most of the time and she cast glances at me which seemed to contain such burning hatred that I was almost afraid. After all, she was called a witch by some. What evil could she do? Why did she seem to despise me so?

We had decided to celebrate the midsummer at Dyfan's camp. There was always a good celebration there and people from all around gathered there for each festival.

Three days before the festival Eiluned and I rode out west as far as the road from Lindum. Although midsummer was very near, Cailleach-Bheur was still intent on swinging her stormy hammer before being overcome by summer. The sky was grey and overcast as we approached the road. A patrolman on his warhorse was coming from the direction of Lindum, his cloak wrapped tightly around him. He looked weird coming slowly, very slowly, down the road with the day so dull. The slight wind flapped our clothing. There was a storm brewing and the horses snorted and shook their heads, As he drew closer, I recognised the horseman as Ystffan Irfon, the soldier we had encountered on our journey from Ceorl's camp to the villa two passings of the full moon ago. 'Hello!' I called to him cheerily.

He stopped and looked at me. He smiled. 'Good day to you. You are Ailin Rhydwyn, are you not?'

'Correct,' I answered. We trotted over to him.

'I see you have become friendly with the woman whose horse was lame.'

'Very,' I said, smiling at Eiluned. 'I don't see many of your companions. Patrolmen usually ride in twos.'

'They did,' Ystffan said, 'Until Artus took half the army to go chasing Wlanca into Gaul. Now he returns to find Mordrawt with an army in the north gradually moving southwards. He will soon be on Artus' own doorstep.'

'Is Artus making no move to drive Mordrawt back?' I asked.

'He has only just returned. He will go against Mordrawt, but too late I fear. Artus's fellowship is crumbling. Many of his best men lie in their graves, many follow Mordrawt including that swine Agrippa who conspired with him. They even tried to say Artus was killed in Armorica to lay claim to leadership.'

'Things look as bleak as this sky,' I commented, looking upwards and around. 'There're few troops on the border, then?' I looked at him again.

'Only those of us you saw that night,' he told me. Then he smiled, 'But the Saxons aren't supposed to know that.'

My spirits were cast down after this conversation. To me only a few months ago Artus had seemed as indestructable as the rocks of these islands themselves, the pillar of strength, the inspiration of Britain. Now he decayed like the cities he governed. We left Ystffan to his lonely patrol and turned for home.

The storm did not hold off for us. The rain fell thick and heavy. There was some thunder and lightning, but we took shelter under trees despite this. It soon became dark, but we decided against making camp for the night and rode through the night back to the villa.

We were back home before daybreak. The villa was in darkness but for one lamp burning on the table in the atrium. Peneli was waiting up for our return. By now the storm had ended. We stabled the horses, and then went in. 'You've been a long while. We feared for your lives in the storm.'

'There was no need,' Eiluned reasssured her.

'Aonghus has been pacing up and down. He's only just gone to bed.'

'We rode a long way. The storm hindered our return,' I explained. I could see by her persistence that she was being suggestive. She knew as well as I that I wouldn't lay a finger uninvited on Eiluned, but for some reason the witch was determined to spoil my happiness. I left the atrium and went to the bedroom where Pedr was snoring.

Both Eiluned and I slept long past the dawning of the new day, only managing to raise ourselves shortly before noon. After dinner I went to my forge and got a nice red fire glowing. Paulus agreed to assist me in the making of a number of spearheads and two new hunting knives which were needed for game and for protection.

Around mid-afternoon I noticed out of the corner of my eye the women across the courtyard gathered round Aonghus. There seemed to be some sort of argument with

Peneli having most of the say in the matter. Aonghus was saying very little. Soon afterwards, the talking stopped abruptly. I looked up from my forge to see Aonghus striding towards me with some sort of determination in his eyes. The heat rising from the forge distorted my vision. I stood up from my bent position over the work. Paulus looked up also.

'Ailin,' Aonghus said, 'Leave her alone.'

'Who?' I asked, knowing damn well what the answer would be.

'Eiluned. Leave her alone.'

I could've crushed his Saxon skull with the hammer in my hand. 'You regard her as being your woman?'

He nodded, and smiled. Smiled out of what? Pride? Or was it the smirk of one who was gloating? No. He couldn't gloat. He couldn't look at me straight, straight in the eye without producing that hideous, childish look. I could have challenged him. I did not. I realised that it would achieve nothing. Eiluned liked, probably loved this spindly Saxon. I held my peace and returned to my forge. Aonghus walked away.

'Are you going to the festival?' Paulus asked. We had planned to leave for Dyfan's camp early the next morning.

'No,' I answered, which was the answer he was expecting.

'Why not?' Paulus wanted to know. I thought it a stupid question. I could see that he was going to try to talk me into going.

'Not much point,' I answered, putting my hammer down and holding the spearhead up to admire it.

'All because of him! Great gods, Ailin why bother? One woman. ONE woman when there are thousands in Britain! One flat-chested woman and you come close to tears. Look at me. I lost one hell of a woman. A REAL woman. Lots of flesh. And I had the misery of losing her to a stronger man than I.'

'Shut up Paulus. I don't want to talk about it. I'm not going and that's that.' I slung the spearhead down and walked out of the workshop, out of the gate brushing passed Pedr who had just entered holding a pair of rabbits by the ears.

I walked up the track and out of the hollow. I went to the side of the stream in which we used to bathe and sat down to contemplate my misfortune. I knew, of course, who was behind all this. Peneli. I could hear her voice now. Only this time I could define the words. She offered the Saxon a challenge, to prove his mettle and protect what was his 'right'. His RIGHT? I asked myself, 'did he have a right to her?' He did. I would have done the same. I felt I should have been the one to offer the challenge. To defend his right in open combat. But it was not my way. Peneli was victorious. But why? What had kindled such hatred in her heart towards me? I had an idea it was something to do with Pedr. Did she blame me? There were so many questions. Few could be resolved. The witch had given Aonghus a strength of will he had not known previously. He felt now that he had been successful in defending himself. But I knew that I had to wait for Eiluned to come to me of her own accord.

I sat pondering until the sunset, until the moon shone. Shortly after sunset, Peneli came to me and sat at my side on the banks of the stream. 'What do you want?' I asked her, trying to sound as though the incident had caused me minor concern. It was stupid of me since my very absence from the villa betrayed my feelings.

'To talk,' the witch replied.

'What about, Peneli?'

'About Pedr,' she answered. I was mildly surprised.

'He no longer wants to marry you. I can't alter that . . .'

'I'm not asking you to. I'm just wondering WHY Pedr no longer loves me.'

'Why not ask Pedr?' I suggested. I was in no mood for other people's problems.

'I know about the way you all laughed at me for wanting him, including him. You knew he didn't really want me.'

'Not all that long before you did,' I argued. I could tell what she was getting at. She was accusing me of spoiling HER romance. The reason she based this on was obvious, she had overthrown me in favour of Pedr, and I was naturally angry at losing a 'prize' such as her. 'Do you think I TOLD Pedr not to marry you?'

'Yes,' she said, uncertainly.

'You're wrong.'

'Am I?' she said and stood up. Then she walked off back down to the villa.

I remember thinking how she flattered herself. True, I had been upset when she passed me over. I don't know why. Was it because of her powers as a witch? I didn't believe that. She simply knew what words to say to the right person at the right time. I had been lonely, and she took me and gave me love. Love was a thing I held so precious then. I no longer do. I think I lost all my fine feelings after that day. There was no place for soft emotions there at that time. A black cloud hung over the whole island of Britain. The men thrived on an understanding of how to HATE. How to hate one's enemy the Saxons, the Picts and the Scots, whoever they might be; how to hate one's brother and fellow man so as to protect what was your own and be braver than the next man in battle; how to hate love so as not to become soft. A warrior who refused to pick up a sword was little use. And I was a warrior. All Celts are warriors. Civilization left when Magnus Maximus led the legions out of Britain. I saw Rome in Eiluned. But more than Rome, I saw in her a divine truth. Something I could not reach out and take. I felt shaken to the foundations. I felt wronged.

I went back down to the villa when I was sure they all slept. They had left the door unbolted for me. I went straight to my bedroom. I undressed and tried to sleep to the rhythm of Pedr's snoring. I didn't sleep until it was nearly morning when I was awakened by Eiluned. She was sitting on the side of my bed. The rest of the household slept. 'Go away,' I said. I felt uneasy. The tongues would wag once more. I was stripped of my happiness, I would not be stripped of my honour, even to a Saxon I considered unworthy to stand in my path.

'Are you coming to the festival?' she asked.

I sat up. 'No. Now leave me alone, Eiluned. Return to your bed.'

'This business with Aonghus, it was little more than a joke. Peneli –'

'I know all about Peneli. Now go!' I spoke in a hoarse whisper. Pedr stirred. 'Go!'

'Why are you so hasty . . .'

'Just go!' I persisted. She went. I slumped back down into my furs. I wanted to weep. I gulped back the painful lump in my throat and tried to sleep, to run and hide in my dreams. After a while I did sleep. And I dreamt I was still riding with Eiluned in the bright sunshine. The sunlight filtered in through the trees, the bees hummed. And the horsemen rode down the road from Lindum two by two, two by two . . . Pedr woke me. There was faint, cold daylight in the bedroom. 'Are you coming?' he asked.

'No,' I said.

He dressed and said: 'You can't lie here all day.'

'Can't I? I'm not going to Dyfan's camp.'

'Have it your way,' he said and left the room.

I didn't go to the festival. Neither did Paulus. As the hroses clattered out of the courtyard, he came to my room and talked me into getting up. I had decided that my time at the villa was coming to an end – but I couldn't think of anywhere to go.

The others returned to the villa a day after the festival had ended. I was anxious to talk to Pedr. It was noon or thereabouts. Pedr retired to the solitude of the study to nurse his headache. He had been very drunk during the whole of the festival. 'What news of Artus?' I asked.

'Who? Artus . . . oh, yes Artus. I heard he's marching North to meet Mordrawt.'

'And Mordrawt, what's he doing?'

'He's retreating to the Wall. Somewhere, some fort Cambog, Cambog something-or-other. I didn't catch all of what they were saying. I was very – '

' – drunk. I know. Was it Camboglanna they were talking about?'

'Yes, that's it Cambog, Cambog . . . what you said.'

I knew the place. I'd been there with my grandfather when I was about fifteen. It was one of the Wall forts. They were unoccupied and rarely patrolled. It was the most hostile border country. Beyond the Wall were the Picts and the Scots settlers. And the kings of the North weren't exactly friendly either.

I thanked Pedr for his information and left him wishing his head would come loose and fall off so as no longer to torment him. I went to my bedroom and picked up my grandfather's sword. I left the scabbard lying on my bed and just took the sword itself to my workshop. I placed it in front of me and studied it. Then I set about making a replica. I spent all afternoon fashioning the blade.

Towards nightfall, Paulus visited the workshop. 'Why are you making a sword, Ailin?' he asked, sounding childishly curious. 'I thought you'd finished making weapons of war when you left Ceorl's camp.'

'I'm going to Camboglanna,' I said.

'Where?' Paulus asked.

'Mordrawt is holding out there against Artus. I'm leaving tomorrow. There's sure to be a battle.'

Paulus was amazed. 'A battle? You, in a battle? You hate warfare.'

'This is different. I'm going. I don't belong here in the sunshine any more.'

'There's no excuse to go out and get yourself killed in a civil war. This is futile, Ailin!'

'I'm going,' I persisted. My mind was made up. I was going to Camboglanna to join Artus' army.

'Then I'm coming too,' he said. I had expected that. I wasn't going to argue, though I did not want him along on my account.

'That's up to you,' I said. He left my workshop. I continued with the sword.

The next morning, the sky was grey again. A drizzle, like the drizzle that had fallen when we first found Aonghus fogged the air. It was cold and my breath steamed as I fitted my spears and weapons of other varieties to my horse. I mounted and was just leaving the stable when Paulus and Pedr entered carrying their gear. No words were exchanged. They silently fixed their stuff to the remaining two horses. Not long afterwards, we clattered and clanked out of the courtyard and up the winding track away from the villa, leaving the gate swinging. I don't know if the others heard us leave. I didn't look back. I wish now that I had, but now is too late.

CHAPTER SIX

Camboglanna

We intended to go to Dyfan's camp and ride with him to Camboglanna. However, we met a group of about six black-horsemen on the Lindum road. Among them was Ystffan Irfon. They were riding to Camboglanna. These were the last few from Durobrivae.

We rode hard to Lindum and reached the town by night-fall. The soldiers there had left apart from one or two of the old men and young boys who stayed to mind the town while the others were away. We stayed the night in Lindum and moved on the next day. We stayed the next night at a small fort between Segelocum and Danum. We left the road the next day in Danum and followed two river valleys for a day and a half, finding our way with the help of various people on the way. The rivers guided us to a point under a day's ride to the fort at Calaractonium. After leaving Calaractonium we began to encounter some pretty rugged country. Up to now the journey had passed without incident apart from our getting lost once or twice due to incorrect interpretation of landmarks. Now however, we were riding into not only a time-consuming loss of direction, but also a certain amount of danger.

It was when we were little more than a day and a half's ride to the north of Calaractonium. Following a road which we had picked up not long after leaving the fort, we were slowed down by the mountainous nature of the terrain. Eventually, the road fell steeply into the valley of a river and we suddenly found ourselves immersed in dense fog. 'Keep to the road,' Ystffan ordered and we obeyed, moving slowly along down towards the river.

The fog seemed to stifle our talk and we moved along with only the clatter of the horses and the clink of our weapons breaking the silence. All else was still as darkness slowly fell to accompany the fog. Then I thought I heard something. I stopped my horse. 'What is it?' Paulus asked. They all halted.

'Listen!' I whispered. They listened. There were voices. They seemed far-off, but you couldn't judge in this grey world. The noise of metal on metal. Laughter.

'Don't make a sound!' Ystffan hissed. He dismounted and handed the reins of his horse to one of the other black-horsemen. He slipped silently off into the fog in the direction of the voices and the accompanying sounds. We waited nervously for his return. After a long wait he came back to the road panting after hard running. 'Celts,' he gasped, 'And Saxons with them, I think. The light's bad, it's hard to see. These Northerners are difficult to tell from Saxons, but I'm pretty sure.'

'What're Saxons doing here in the middle of Elmet? We're seven day's ride from Saxon territory,' said Onllwyn, one of the soldiers.

'Why do they join with Celts?' another wanted to know.

'How many are there?' Paulus enquired. 'Are they on foot?'

'There're about twenty and five. All on foot, not even packhorse.'

'Do you think we should move on or remain here and see what happens, Ystffan?' I asked. Ystffan was the most experienced among us. We accepted him as the leader of our party.

'I say we stay and see how things turn out. They're getting ready to make camp for the night. Artus'll want to hear about this. It's a funny situation. I don't understand what's going on.' And we all nodded in agreement.

We made our camp on the roadside. In the middle of the night when we were sure they slept for the most part, we left Paulus with the horses and the remaining eight of us slipped silently along the valley. I had armed myself with my sword. One of our number carried a bow and three arrows and another two were armed with long war-spears; the others carried daggers.

The war-band (as they surely were from the amount of weapons they carried) was camped not far from the river itself. Four guards patrolled the camp and the others snored as their fires burned. I stuck close to Pedr, even though Ystffan had told us to split up. Long before we reached a point where the men could be defined clearly through the fog, we halted and stayed in that position for some time lying on our bellies in the wet grass. Then Ystffan darted swiftly and silently away from the line we formed, his back arched and his sword outstretched like the nose of a hound sniffing towards the enemy, as we regarded them. Shortly afterwards another scuttled after him armed with the bow. Pedr and I stayed where we were and watched anxiously. The two black forms sped swiftly towards one of the guards. The archer diverted the guard's attention. Ystffan moved into the space between the guard and the camp as the archer drew him away with a few noises. He was careful to remain out of sight. I realised that they were attempting to capture the guard. We prayed to all our gods that the other three guards wouldn't notice right away that one of their number was missing. The tension grew unbearable as Ystffan sneaked up on the guard from the rear. He was almost upon him when the guard heard him and spun round. My heart missed a beat and it seemed as though all was lost. But Ystffan was not so nervous. The tip of his sword rested over the guard's breast before he had time to lower his spear. Ystffan put his finger to his lips and the guard obeyed. We all sighed with relief. Whilst the archer covered their withdrawel, Ystffan and his captive moved back towards us after the man had been disarmed. When the three reached us, we stood up and Pedr caught the guard's spear which Ystffan threw over to him. He went back to our camp with the prisoner.

Paulus looked at the man in amazement. 'You snatched a prisoner?' There was no need to answer since we obviously had. The man was only slightly taller than Paulus. He was a Northerner, short and very dark of hair and wrapped in lugubrious furs. His spear had been his only weapon.

'Who are you?' Ystffan asked whilst Pedr restrained the man. He offered little resistance.

'I am Farquhar,' the Northerner replied in his broad Northern accent, barely understandable.

'From where?' Ystffan asked sharply. 'Far North?'

'Aye.'

'Why are you here? Why are there Saxons with you?'

The man was reluctant to answer. Pedr put his sword under the man's chin and pushed his head upwards with it. 'Alright!' Farquhar gasped. 'We are sent by Mordrawt to harrass forces coming from the south to prevent them from reaching Combaglanna. The Saxons are Dierans.'

'Diera is allied with Mordrawt?' I asked him.

'Aye.'

'How many such war-bands are there?' Ystffan queried.

'Not many.'

'HOW many?'

The man strained his terrified eyes down to look at Pedr's blade. 'Five, six . . . seven at the most.'

'The main force must be at Camboglanna,' one of the soldiers said.

'We can handle this bunch,' said another.

Pedr lowered his blade to the man's back. 'What about this one?' Ystffan raised his sword to strike at the man's throat. I caught his arm. 'No, Ystffan. You can't.'

'Do you suggest we let him run back to his friends? We can't keep him, he has no horse. Would you give him yours?' He didn't give me chance to answer. He pushed me off his arm and modified the same movement to bring the blade down onto the trembling Northerner's throat. The man gurgled and blood spurted and spewed. He collapsed to the wet grass, making the fog swirl. Ystffan wiped the blade on the sleeve of his jerkin and then thrust it into his scabbard. I was speechless at the sight of this brutality. Not even Ceorl would have done such a thing in cold blood. But then, before it had been peace, now it was war. Ystffan seemed undisturbed. 'Now we must attack,' he said. 'We'll go in on horseback. That'll give us eighteen bodies against twenty and four, that is,' he looked at me, 'If you're coming, Ailin.' His voice was calm and friendly again. I nodded slowly and unsurely. 'We must be quick. The fog's beginning to clear.'

We mounted our horses, first removing all arms we wouldn't require and leaving them hidden near the camp. We strapped on our shields and the soldiers their helmets also. The blackhorsemen favoured their spears as their primary weapons, with swords at their sides for close-combat. Paulus and I did the same, thinking that these men should know best. Pedr, however, favoured his sword only.

We trotted slowly and for the most part silently until we could just see a few dark forms moving about the camp. They had obviously just missed Farquhar. We broke into a gallop. The enemy suddenly looked up, when we could see them clearly, Ystffan let out a blood-chilling war-cry and the other soldiers did the same. Spears levelled we rode into the surprised Northern and Saxon camp. Our first charge was un-stoppable. Spears shattered shields and warriors fell to be trampled beneath the horse's hooves.

We turned to charge again. The enemy formed into a triangular battle-formation and the soldiers divided equally on either side. Paulus and I followed Ystffan in and Pedr went in on the other side nearest the river. This time the charge slammed into the enemy and wavering, almost stopped, though it did serve to shatter their formation. Swords rang as they slid from their scabbards and flashed in the light from the dying campfires. Blood and brains spattered the grass and matted the furs which men on either side wore. A man went sprawling into the fire and screamed as a glowing stick thrust up his nose. A great Saxon lumbered towards me, his weapon knocked from his hand. He reached out with his bare hands to grab my leg. I could have struck him down, but he was unarmed . . . Pedr flashed by and the man fell, his head flopped, bled, tore and rolled. After this I was determined to kill. The sight and smell of blood and guts turned my brain. I wanted a prize for myself. I threw my spear into the confusion of the battle and drew my sword. I dug my heels into my horse and slashed into the remaining enemy. I struck two down and not long afterwards it was all over. Nine of us on horseback stood in a tight circle around a heap of dead. More bodies were littered around outside the circle. One of the soldiers coughed. Blood came out of his mouth and he fell onto the heap of bodies next to his horse. Onllwyn dismounted and inspected the body. 'Dead,' he reported.

None of us moved. The horses stood still. I leaned forward and rested my arm on the horse's neck, wiping the sweat from my brow with my other, my right arm the hand of which still clasped my sword. The handle was warm in my palm. I sheathed the blade, not caring to wipe away the blood and pieces of gut as the soldiers did. It felt like the way you feel after half a night of love-making. The desire for a woman's body once satisfied retreats to its lair leaving the exhausted body. It felt the same. Only it was blood-lust that had been satisfied. After a while, we returned slowly to our camp at the roadside.

The next morning the fog lifted. The blackhorsemen returned to the scene of the battle and collected up as many of the deadmen's arms as they could carry. I did not go near, but we could see, Pedr, Paulus and I. It was then, after a night's sleep that I realised the horror of the previous night. We had killed every last one of them. We had lost one of ours whom we buried. The rest we left to the mercy of the crows.

When we had finished with the remnants of the skirmish, we went on our way, following the road. We passed through Olicana next, a small Roman village accompanied by an overgrown fortress with crumbling ramparts. All was deserted, since the Romans had left. Through this town a river flowed, and it was the forested valley of this river which we followed until we found the road to Virosidum which joined the valley where the river swung gently North-West. Large areas of the valley were clear of the forest and were occupied by scattered huts and farmlands. The forested areas, however, were dense and dark. These were inhabited by the people of the woods, a strange people with slender bodies as small as the other Northerners but not thickset. These people could blend into the background of the forest. We knew that they watched us. Paulus saw flashes of sunlight on objects moving through the trees. I myself saw a flicker of long dark hair curl around the trees and vanish into their depths. We kept clear and muttered charms to ourselves to ward off these strangers' powers.

It took us a day and a half to reach the settlement and fortress of Virosidum. We rode throughout the night, not wishing to make camp in the forest. The woodspeople were many and poor, and perhaps followers of Mordrawt like the other Northerners we had encountered. But they did not trouble us while we were awake and moving. They are shy like the animals of their woodlands. Paulus, who had no liking for the darkness, insisted that it was not the woodspeople we saw but the woodnymphs who he had heard many stories about. They were the friends of witches. . . . We laughed, but only half from amusement.

We only rested until mid-afternoon at Virosidum and then we rode North. Not far from Virosidum, we were directed by a farmer to follow the valley of yet another river which twisted and turned gradually northwards for another day's ride until it flowed near to another road passing under a bridge overshadowed by a Roman fort called Lavatrae.

We took the road west for a couple of days and met up with some more of Artus' soldiers at a fort on the road called Bravoniacum. Along with these men, (Northerners by the look of them), we turned onto a more northerly heading road. We travelled along this until we reached another fort. Here we rested for the night. The next morning we set off along the road. During the day we crossed three stretches of water. Not far beyond the third we left the road and struck west again, towards the sunset. In this area we saw a lot of men on their way to Camboglanna. We joined up with them and we numbered about thirty when we finally arrived at the place where Artus' army faced the Wall and the extensive ramparts of the fort at Camboglanna.

It was dusk when we arrived. Torches were lit and soldiers gathered around their campfires. Though it was summer, the North did not grow a great deal warmer.

Ystffan left us and went to report what had happened on the road to Olicana with the Northern war-band. Pedr and I shared a fire with the others we met on the way. Paulus did not feel like sleeping and so took the first guard duty for the night.

The next morning, a watery sunlight paled the sky. I woke early and walked through the sleeping men to take a clearer look at the stronghold in which most of Mordrawt's army slept. The decaying Hadrian's Wall flowed over the hills towards sunrise and sunset. The walls of the fort were high and grey-brown and forbidding. Solitary guards patrolled them, black against the morning sky with their cloaks flapping in the chill breeze, the dim sunlight running over the heads of their spears like a trickle of mountain water. I heard footsteps behind me. It was one of the blackhorsemen from the Lindum road, Ignatius, I think, was his name. 'The air smells of men's blood this morning,' he said. To my nostrils it smelled clean, fresh.

'Today we will fight the battle?' I asked.

'Yes, today. You never know how or when it starts. You're suddenly in it. Only the commanders ever know.'

I looked towards the guards walking up and down the walls of the fort. Other figures began to appear on the ramparts. I heard voices from all along our own lines. The men were waking, one became aware that the battlefield was stirring into life.

Pedr and Paulus walked to my side. 'We've had orders to mount up,' Pedr informed me. I nodded and we all three walked to the place where our horses were tied to a long rope between two trees. We placed our weapons on them and then mounted ourselves after first untying them.

We trotted the horses a short distance towards the fort. Then we halted in a neat line. The trees where the camp had been made lay behind us. There were only a few foot-soldiers walking among them and the ashes of our fires smouldered.

I craned this way and that to look at our position. I saw that the horsemen were in two distinct groups, each covering one flank of the attack. The infantry bustled about in an elongated straggling mass in the centre with the archers at the fore. There were about three score infantrymen. They were an assorted lot, mostly peasants dressed in their bright woollen clothes. They talked excitedly and their weapons clinked and jangled as they shifted nervously.

The mounted men seemed more calm and disciplined. We were almost the last to arrive bringing the total number of the cavalry to about a hundred and fifty. Of these, about seventy were blackhorsemen mounted on the mighty Northern cross-breeds. Others, like myself and my two companions, were mounted on the same horses but we were not part of Artus's main army. Others were mounted on lesser horses. It was a sad remnant of the former glory of Artus's army. There were only a few old soldiers in the infantry that Artus had inherited from Ambrosius Aurelianus whereas there used to be many. Their sons and grandsons, like me, had reverted largely to the more native, Celtic ways.

It seemed we waited for an eternity for anything to happen. Then we heard fast hoofbeats and we leaned forwards to gaze around the next man along the line. Ystffan was coming back after being away all night. He was clad in full battle-dress, leathers and chain-mail and was armed with his cavalry sword, the spatha and a long war-spear from which flapped a number of streamers, with which it was the custom for the soldiers to decorate their spears. Ystffan shouted to our end of the line. 'Artus is riding out to try to reason with Mordrawt. No man will draw his sword, lower his spear or stray from his position until further orders. If treachery occurs, then we ride into battle. With luck and God's help we will be able to return home without the clash of swords!' Then Ystffan rode to my side.

His helmet gleamed in the sunlight. He did not speak. None of us wanted to talk. It felt like a thousand maggots crawled in my belly. The horses snorted in anticipation. Then suddenly a wave of chatter ran along the line and ceased as suddenly as it started. Artus was riding by. The sound of his horse's hooves on the boggy turf seemed slow and calculated. The breeze fluttered the matted manes of the horses and my own hair.

He was a large man, very large. He was clad in battle-dress, his shining bronze helmet surmounted by the likeness of a dragon that must have been fashioned in gold. His shield had a cross on it of bronze also. His spear was long with a shaft the width of a man's wrist, colourfully decorated and the spearhead shining. On his left side I saw the hilt of his famous sword, reputably forged in the waters of the best forging cale in the whole of Britain. He rode by on his great white steed. It was the whitest horse I had ever seen, but I had only seen a few in my whole life. The war-horses of Britain were almost always the black cross-breeds. He went by and the chain mail jingled. It was the first and last time I had seen him really close. There was a look of admiration in all our eyes.

We were close to the end of the line of the army. At the end of the line he turned and rode faster back in the direction from which he had come. His face was lined with age and beaten by the weather. He wore a bushy beard which clung to his chin like lichen. It was streaked with grey as was the fringe which hung below his helmet. His eyes were set back in large sockets below which hung the pockets of wrinkled flesh, and lines like the feet of birds spread from the corners of the brown eyes so that it looked as though he squinted. But he did not. His eyes were alert as though a fire burned brightly behind each one.

Artus joined two of his men in front of the army. I saw a colourful clattering line of horsemen spew from the fort. I guessed that Mordrawt was leading them. The line snaked down the embankments and drew towards Artus and his two commanders, probably Cai and Bedwyr. 'If only Wlanca were here,' Ystffan said between his teeth. I continued to watch.

Mordrawt's horsemen broke off and lined up to face our army. The two armies were about equal in the strength of their cavalry, but I couldn't tell how many on foot there were in the fort. I could see some archers on the battlements, and there was even a band of picts making barbaric noises and gesticulating with their javelins.

Mordrawt and two others approached Artus and his commanders in the centre of the battlefield. I was suddenly aware of the smell of peat and heather. The sky grew colder and the breeze more blustery. We waited. They talked. They talked for so long that it seemed they must have agreed. Then . . . then I'm not sure what happened. The cavalry on the other flank charged on both sides. The men in the middle suddenly withdrew to their own armies. Artus was shouting and waving. I could see he was trying vainly to halt the charge. But he could not. The two wings clashed together and I saw the horsemen opposite us coming forwards. We charged. I felt sudden fear grip my stomach. I yelled with the rest of them to rid myself of the fear. I levelled my spear and my thoughts raced. I thought of Pedr and Paulus at my side, of Aonghus and Eiluned . . . Then we were almost upon the enemy, and my thoughts turned to directing the point of my spear to strike. I had in my sight a man charging confidently towards me. He was one of the rebel blackhorse soldiers. I wondered if I seemed as fearsome to him as he did to me. Then we clashed and the horses on both sides reared up and clumps of turf spattered from beneath their hooves. There was a roar as the weapons battered on shields. My own adversary almost unseated me but I managed to deflect his course with the shaft of my spear which I then rammed hard onto his horse's flank so that the animal leaped and shifted aside. I realised I had to rid myself of the cumbersome spear and I threw it at the back of one of the enemy who was engaged in hacking at one of our lads. I didn't halt to see the outcome, but drew my blade and began hacking myself. The walls of the fort were obscured by men and horses. Paulus and Pedr were also lost to my view somewhere in the thick of the battle. A man who had fallen from his horse stumbled through the forest of blades and hooves, guarding his face with his arms, trying to get out of the way. He crumbled beneath my sword and his blood stained the grass and was soaked up by the peaty soil. The horses riding over him scattered his brains. I warded off blows with my shield and struck out blindly. Then both sides wavered and pulled back.

As we re-grouped we saw the litter of horse and men in the space we left. Some were still alive. I realised how hot it was in the thick of the fight and was thankful for the breeze. Then we went headlong in again, stumbling over the sprawling bodies some of whom were our own and still alive. Arrows flew bothways overhead and we ducked beneath our shields, thrusting with our swords. Blood and bone spat everywhere. A sword came down and cut through my jerkin into my arm. I lashed out with my sword and the man who made the cut fell beneath my horse's hooves. The cut was only shallow, but it smarted. I received several similar wounds throughout the course of the battle.

The battle lasted all day until men on either side were too tired to continue. Finally, the infantry overran the fort and Mordrawt's men gave up. But we had not won. Stunned by the realisation that I was alive, I had lived through the battle, I withdrew to the trees and dismounted. I wiped my blade and sheathed the sword. I ached all over, especially in my groin where I had been across the back of my horse all day long.

Pedr came riding towards me. 'They say Artus has fallen,' he called. I was mildly perturbed.

'Where's Paulus?' I wanted to know as Pedr halted and dismounted with a groan.

'I thought you'd know. I've not seen him.'

Reluctantly, I remounted and rode out onto the field to look for my other friend. The darkness began to close in. Pedr followed me. We split up for the search. It was I who found him. I saw him lying on the top of an elongated heap of corpses, but Paulus was alive and moaning. I dismounted and called to Pedr. He came over and leapt from his horse. We bent down to inspect our friend. There was a stink of sweat, the sweetish smell of blood and the spilled intestines of men. Paulus was clasping his side. We removed his hands to find that his tunic was soaked in blood. His old wound had pulled open. We lifted him carefully. Pedr offered to carry him whilst I led the horses.

We went back to the trees and set about binding up the wound. 'We'd better not burn it again. It didn't do much good last time,' I said.

'I'll go and find somebody who can help him,' said Pedr and he got on one of the horses and trotted away.

Whilst Pedr was looking for someone with a knowledge

of medicine I lit a fire and lay Paulus' body on some furs. He lapsed into fitful sleep.

Pedr returned alone. 'I can't find anybody to help,' he reported, 'But someone suggested we take him to the woodspeople.'

'That's a long way to travel with him, and then we might not see any woodspeople,' I said anxiously. Pedr dismounted.

'What else can we do? The woodspeople have the knowledge of how to cure such a wound. The woods cover much of the land not far south. The woodspeople themselves offered to help Artus.'

I nodded in agreement. 'Alright. I'll construct a litter to carry him on. We'll not sleep until we find woodspeople to help him.'

A little later we set off south. I hoped that the woodspeople still lingered in that valley near Virosidum, nearly four days away to the south.

CHAPTER SEVEN

The Dryads

We rode south for three days, hardly resting at all. Paulus's condition grew steadily worse. At first he groaned a little when the litter skipped over large bumps in the road, but now as we approached Lavatrae, he was in continuous agony and never came out of a delirious state for a day and a night. He could no longer travel. And so we decided to bring the woodspeople to him. Pedr stayed at Lavatrae with Paulus and I set off in the direction of Virosidum.

I tried to keep up a fairly fast pace. I rode for a day and a night through forested valleys looking for any sign of the woodspeople before I reached Virosidum. I didn't see any people but for Northerners. Whilst on the way the realisation struck me of what Artus's fall in battle meant to the island of Britain. Only Mordrawt was left, and I didn't know that for sure. Paulus had babbled something about Artus killing Mordrawt with his own sword. If that was true there seemed to be no-one who could take over repelling the enemies of Britain. I thought about the villa, and where it lay east of the Lindum road. I feared for Eiluned's safety. I made up my mind to return as soon as the woodspeople had cured Paulus, if I could find one among these people with a vast knowledge of healing in time. Only they could help Paulus. The wound was diseased and oozed blood and yellow pus frequently, so that death seemed to radiate from it.

I didn't pause in Virosidum, but rode straight through the village and off down the road towards the valley of the river which flowed down to Olicana. In this valley I rode slowly. This was where we had caught brief glimpses of the woodspeople before. I searched the trees now thinking about what Paulus had said about the woodnymphs, the DRYADS as they were called in the ancient myths of the Romans. I had almost given up hope when I spotted a small, crude hut in a clearing in the forest. It was made from branches and logs and plastered with mud and dung in places. A small mongrel hound lay near the door which was covered with a leather apron. A goat was tied to the building. I advanced towards the building. As my horse nosed into the clearing, the goat began to make a noise and the dog got to its feet and went into the hut. A woman came out. She was young, but the weather and the poverty had etched out lines on her face. She had hair which under the matted filth must have been the same colour as Merriam's. The woman was clothed in black woollen fabric and a wolf-skin coat which she must have valued. Her face was thin and the cheekbones protruded, stretching the weather-beaten skin. 'What . . . what is it you want, soldier.'

I came straight to the point. There was little time to waste. 'Can you heal?'

'You are not hurt. Where are you from? Camboglanna? Our menfolk are at Camboglanna.'

'I am from Camboglanna. I have a friend. Only the woodspeople can cure his wound. He is dying.'

She looked at me steadily for a moment then called inside the hut. 'Wenda!' Another woman emerged. She was not like this woman I had first spoken to. Wenda was the same build, but beautiful. Her hair hung in curls and brushed her face which was smooth as silk from the east. She wore no furs, just the woollen fabric which was died green and black. 'The soldier requires our help.' And Wenda smiled briefly.

'Can you save my friend's life?' I asked.

'What of repayment? I have not eaten for a day and a night, neither has Wenda. We are poor, we people of the woods.'

'My other friend is the best huntsman in all Britain. I will give you furs also, if you will help.'

The women looked at each other. Wenda nodded. 'We will heal your friend. My name is Hannah. Where is your friend?'

'A few days' ride to the North at an old fort called Lavatrae. Do you have a horse?' I wished that I had brought our other horse along.

'They have horses in the village, down the valley. We can steal a horse from there.'

I was surprised at the way Hannah calmly stated she could steal a horse. But steal a horse the two of them did. They told me to wait at their hut and they returned after dark with a sturdy little animal from the village. 'It was very easy,' Hannah said. 'He was just tied to a fence. We simply untied him and brought him here.'

'Were there no guards?'

'Yes,' they both said, and Wenda added; 'But they didn't see us.'

And so we set off, along with one goat and one dog, back North towards Lavatrae. I found their company amusing. They were not at all like the traditional woodspeople we had heard of. These women were happy and pleasant and laughed a lot. But Wenda was strange. Her eyes had a veil across them so that they were not clear, you could not communicate with her through her eyes as you could most people. But then the main thing for me was to get back to Paulus and let the woodspeople heal his wound.

We arrived at Lavatrae after riding hard for four days. Pedr came out onto the road. His face was grim. I feared that Paulus had died and rode quickly towards him. 'He's grown worse,' was all Pedr said when I reached him.

'Worse?'

'He is in constant pain even when he is not moving. The wound oozes with filth and blood. The flesh of his side has turned red and black.'

I dismounted. 'I have brought the woodspeople.'

'It may be too late.'

Hannah and Wenda cantered up shortly. 'I thank you for coming,' Pedr said. 'Come this way.'

We went into the fort and made our way to the praetorium building, leaving the horses in the forum. Paulus was lying on the furs near the wall opposite the door. He writhed in pain and the dressing on the wound was stained scarlet from his blood. He had grown very thin.

Hannah and Wenda went softly to his side and knelt down to examine the wound. 'It's bad,' Hannah said.

'Can you heal it?' I asked.

'Perhaps,' Hannah said and she stood up. 'We will gather the herbs.' And they left us. They returned shortly afterwards carrying armfuls of plants and weeds. They set them down on the floor of the room and sorted through them, selecting the correct amounts of the different herbs. Then they ground them in an earthenware pot from the camp and boiled them in water. The brownish liquid was strained off and forced down Paulus's throat. Soon afterwards he stopped squirming from the pain. 'He sleeps now,' Hannah said.

They prepared more herbs and made the thick slimy stuff that Peneli had put on Aonghus's wound. Or I think it was that anyway. But unlike Peneli, they did not burn the wound. They cleaned it inside and out with cloth and herbs and then put the green stuff all over it and bound it tightly. The wound bled no more after that.

They stayed and nursed him for days. Paulus grew quite fond of Hannah when he returned to his former self, but she returned his affection with laughter and jokes.

Pedr hunted the boar and we gave a certain amount of his catch to our friends as I had promised, along with a number of furs.

Then there was the beautiful Wenda. I was attracted to her for many reasons. She seemed somehow innocent, though she laughed as much as Hannah and her speech was much the same. But Wenda was an enigma, with her eyes that betrayed nothing and the soft skin on her face, so unlike the skin of Hannah, who was typical of the woods-people in her appearance.

I stood with Wenda one night on the battlements, leaning on the wall and looking out across the tortured landscape of these high-lands.

'When will Paulus be well again?' I enquired, turning to look into her face.

'You can't expect him to be whole straight away. It will be another passing of the full moon yet.'

It was a full moon that night. I thought of the villa and Eiluned. Artus had fallen, the Saxons would rampage across Britain soon. The villa was in the path of that fury. I knew that I had to go there.

'Can we leave Paulus with you? I have to go South very soon. Pedr will want to come too. We'll return for him.'

'I do not like this place. It is full of ghosts, they watch from all around.'

'Then take him to your forest. Surely he can travel slowly to the valley. We must travel with all haste not far south of Lindum.'

She thought for a moment. 'Very well. When do you plan to leave?'

'Maybe two days,' I answered. Then we fell silent. I suddenly knew what had eluded me in Wenda. The light curling hair, the soft skin and the eyes had the look of civilization about them. There was Roman in her. There was something, something (I hardly dared to admit it to myself), something of Eiluned within Wenda. Her slight figure and the hue of her hair, that skin. But the eyes still concealed much and lacked the happiness in Eiluned's eyes. 'Are your parents alive?' I asked, trying to discover from whence the Roman in her came.

'Aye, they're alive.'

'I see in you that one of your parents is not of the woods.'

'My father is from the South of Britain. My parents live in Aquae Sulis. I like the forest better. Where are your parents, Ailin?'

'Dead,' I answered. 'Pedr's are in Armorica, and Paulus's are dead also.' And again the silence fell. I wondered how long it had been since I had taken a woman. It must have been last summer, at the midsummer feast when the tribespeople danced and sang and ate and drank for three whole days. At that time I had been betrothed to Peneli and we had been as free as the rest, kissing and holding each other. I had lain with her then. Now she seemed only a shadowy memory, for I had Wenda with me, and the past seemed to be moving away faster each day. I turned Wenda to face me and moved forwards to kiss her. For a moment, the curtain withdrew from her eyes and a speck of light like a star burned there and sparkled. Before my lips touched hers, she pulled free from my arms and my gaze. The veil fell again and she said goodnight, and left me to go to her bed.

The following afternoon, after talking to Pedr, I told Paulus our intention to leave. 'You're not leaving me!' he protested, 'I can sit across a horse! My wound is well. I am coming.'

'No, Paulus,' I said firmly, 'It will be a month before the wound is safe to abuse. Hannah and Wenda will take you to the forest. You like Hannah, don't you?'

'Of course I like her, but she only laughs at me, she doesn't take me seriously. I'm not going to beg for the affections of a woodswoman. I will ride with you.'

'Sorry, Paulus, I will not let you come for your own sake. You will stay with Hannah and Wenda. Understood?'

'You cannot tell me –'

'I'm telling you now. You are not coming and that's final.' And with that I got up and walked out of the building.

I found Pedr exploring the old granary. The women were

with him. 'Paulus is being awkward,' I said. Pedr turned around.

'What's new?'

'I shouldn't think he'll be able to argue very effectively,' I turned to Hannah, avoiding looking into Wenda's face. 'Can you manage an argumentative patient?'

Hannah laughed. 'He is too small to trouble me or Wenda greatly.'

'Don't tell him that! Thanks for everything.'

'My belly is full and my body is warm, it is payment enough.'

Pedr and I set off the following morning away from the road and the fort in the direction of Virosidum. It was very early and when we vacated the fort of Lavatrae the others slept. But we had only traversed a few gradus when I heard a familiar voice from behind. 'Ailin! Pedr! Wait for me you pair of fools! You can't leave me behind!'

We halted and turned our heads. 'Ignore him,' I said to Pedr. Paulus was on foot, struggling with a bundle of furs and stumbling over the rough land. We turned away and rode on.

'Come back!' he yelled at the top of his voice, 'Come back or I shall walk back to the villa and kill myself in the process!'

He meant it. I stopped and looked back to see him come stumbling after us. He suddenly cried out and fell. His wound! The thoughts raced through my mind. My old friend, with whom I had spent so many merry times, and whose stubbornness had made us so angry on so many occasions. I did not want to leave him behind, yet knew it was best for him. And now, here he was, as awkward as ever, refusing to be left behind. I shouted to Pedr and galloped back to where he lay. I got down from my horse and looked at him. 'Paulus,' I said, bending down. He rolled over and grinned.

'I tripped.' He struggled to stand up and pain racked his face. He slumped down again. 'I'm coming, Ailin.'

I sighed heavily and helped him up and onto my horse. I climbed on behind him and sped after Pedr who waited ahead. Then we began our homeward journey south.

CHAPTER EIGHT

The Return

The return journey did Paulus no good. By good fortune the wound didn't open again, but by the time we reached Lindum Paulus had fallen into a fever. I wished that I had hardened my heart and taken him back to the woodswomen at the fort of Lavatrae.

We stayed in Lindum for a couple of days. The place was almost deserted but for confused military men and the few people who had not left either because they did not want to leave their homes or because they were fools and didn't realise the threat from the Saxons.

During our stay, the town suffered two small attacks from ambitious war-bands coming from the North-East who found that they had met with little resistance on the borderlines of the far North. I hoped that the Saxons further South had not got the message yet. It would take a little time for the legend of the blackhorsemen to dwindle in their hearts.

Ourselves, we were reasonably safe in Lindum. The two war-bands were repelled without much loss. The Saxons cared nothing for the towns, I heard that they believed them to have been built by giants.

We left on the morning of the third day we had been in Lindum and set off down the road. Paulus condition had improved somewhat during the short rest in Lindum.

The road was crowded with refugees. It was hard to believe that there were so many people East of the border who were Britons. We paid little attention to them and rode fast on our journey. We didn't take the short cut which Eiluned had shown us because of the danger from marauding Saxons. We kept to the highway until we reached a point where to ride directly towards the rising sun would bring us to the villa.

It was drawing towards nightfall when we nervously approached the rim of the hollow in which the villa stood. We had sighted no Saxons but knew they were close, perhaps some lurked in the villa itself. But there were no lights showing below. Quite suddenly I feared for Eiluned and could hold back no longer. Boldly I hurried down the track which led to the gate.

The gate swung on its hinges, just as it had done when we had left for Camboglanna. We rode slowly through the gate and halted in the cobbled yard. 'Anyone here?' I called. Only the shadow of an echo replied. We all dismounted. Pedr walked towards the house and I followed lending the assistance of my shoulder to Paulus.

As Pedr stepped in after pushing the door open, I half expected to be confronted with four mutilated corpses spread across the floor. But the grey stone floor was covered only by a thin layer of dust which barely showed up in the fading daylight.

Pedr found a candle and lit it with his flint and tinder which he carried tucked inside his belt. The flickering light made the shadows lurch around the atrium. The table and chairs were empty. The homely wall-paintings seemed eerie. The place seemed stranger now, as it did on my very first visit. I felt as though I had been away from the villa for an eternity, and the others had withered away; died in their beds and fallen to dust.

The bedrooms and the study were also quite empty but for the furniture. The bedframes had been stripped of the furs.

We lit a fire in the brazier in the atrium and decided to spend the night there. I went out to the workshop and looked around the forge with a candle. There I found grandfather's sword where I had left it when I made the sword which had served me so well as Camboglanna. Grasping the sword, memories flooded back to my mind like water to a dry throat. I could remember when I detested the thought of having to go into battle and slay an enemy. It seemed such a far-off memory now as though it was not I who had ever thought that at all. It was as if I were pondering the character of a close kinsman and not MYSELF. I thought of the noise of the battle of Camboglanna, the blood and the heat and my tormented body as I rode my horse weaving in and out of the thick of the fighting again and again and again. I thought of Farquhar, the Northerner whom Ystffan Irfon killed in that valley before the skirmish. There was death on my hands, in my arms, my heart and mind.

I returned to the house, carrying the sword. We slept on

the floor that night, wrapped in our furs and gathered around the brazier.

'We'll have to leave in the morning,' Pedr said, his voice piercing the darkness.

'Where do we go?' Paulus wanted to know.

'Where do you think Eiluned and the rest have gone?' I asked.

'Fled to the west, of course,' Pedr said.

'Do you want to find her, Ailin?' Paulus asked me.

I nodded, though he couldn't see me in the darkness he knew the answer. 'Maybe she's gone to Ceorl's camp,' I suggested.

'Maybe,' Pedr agreed. 'Do you want to go there?'

'We've no quarrel with Ceorl these days. We'll go to his camp tomorrow,' I said.

'That's alright with me,' Paulus said. 'I wonder what happened to Ystffan.'

It seemed out of place to wonder at Ystffan's fate. 'What has Ystffan to do with Ceorl?' Pedr asked.

'I was just thinking about the soldiers,' Paulus replied. 'I wonder what DID happen to him. Did he fall at Cambo-glanna?'

'I didn't see him fall,' I said. 'Did you see him, Pedr?'

'No,' Pedr answered. 'If he's still alive he's probably gone south like the rest of Artus' army apart from deserters. The soldiers at Lindum are withdrawing to Glevum, Aquae and Corinium so some of them said. Perhaps some just hoped they were going anyway.'

'I heard say they were standing to defend the border,' Paulus put in.

'What border?' Pedr sniggered.

I thought about what Pedr had said; IF Ystffan Irfon was still alive. IF. It seemed somehow strange to say IF when considering whether a man was alive or dead, not strong enough. I don't quite know why; human nature? It was like the time when a man was dragged from a river and people asked IF he were drowned. Like the time we found Paulus lying on the heap of corpses at Camboglanna and as I approached him I had wondered IF he was alive. And Pedr's voice telling me that Aonghus was alive when we found him on the track leading up to Ceorl's camp. It all seemed so long ago. So much had happened in so short a time.

'I wonder if Merriam's fled west too,' Paulus said, almost to himself.

'I expect so,' I answered. 'But I wonder if Ceorl's gone with her.'

'Can't imagine him staying for very long without his woman . . .' Pedr mused.

'Do you still desire her, Paulus?' I asked.

'No,' he lied.

'I'm hungry,' Pedr complained, ever the practical one, rolling over in his furs. 'Did we bring any food from Lindum?'

'A little,' Paulus answered. 'But I think we should save it for the morning.'

'Very well,' Pedr said and rolled over again. Then he stood up, throwing off his furs. 'I'm not tired. I'm going to get dressed and see if there's any ale in the kitchen.' And he did so. He returned from the kitchen with two large jars of ale and set them down on the floor near the brazier. He pulled out one of the stoppers and took a long drink from the jar. Then he set it down again and wiped his mouth with the back of his hand. His face was mostly in the shadow, but the brazier illuminated the look in his eyes. 'I've waited long for that,' he said as though his life depended on the ale. Pedr took a peculiar delight in getting himself befuddled. 'Want a drink, my friends?' he asked us. We sat up and he passed the pitcher round. The ale went round and round and round until both bottles were dry, and we fell dead asleep, not drunk, but feeling contentment and ease. I was glad to rest easy that night.

The realisation that I was cold woke me. I opened my eyes and stared into Pedr's glassy eyes. I managed to sit up and leaned over to give Paulus a shake. He woke with a groan. The pale dawn light crept across the floor as we straightened our clothes. 'God give me strength to move!' Paulus said, holding his wound. 'This morning I'm as stiff as an oak.'

We fetched the horses from the stable where we had left them the night before and set about loading the furs and other belongings onto them. Then we heard them. We heard the clatter of arms, voices shouting and laughing. We stopped what we were doing and concentrated on the sounds coming from the forest side of the hollow. The next thing we knew, the Saxons had emerged from the forest and were crawling around the rim of the hollow like ants as the sun began to glow above the tops of the trees.

'Stay out of sight!' I called and we ran inside the open stable door.

Now the Saxons surrounded the hollow and seemed to be waiting to see if they could see any sign of life. I thought to myself that this was the end of the road. The Saxons were advancing to the border and the villa would be their first taste of 'the guts of the land'.

'This is it,' Paulus said quietly.

'Maybe we can slip past them,' I said desperately, trying to give myself hope. I wished that the house would move so that I could see the other side of the hollow. From what I could see, there appeared to be about thirty of the Saxons around us. That would be ten Saxons for every one of us.

'We have a chance,' Pedr said suddenly. 'I'll go out and clear the trackway on my horse. Then I'll act as a decoy and draw them off while you two clear out.'

'Don't talk such rubbish! You'd be killed,' I argued.

'Perhaps,' Pedr agreed. 'But I can't see the sense in all of us dying, as we surely will if they get their hands on us.'

'We'll go down together,' Paulus said, but as he said the last word, Pedr shot like an arrow from the stable and ran to one of the horses. I dived after him, trying to catch his legs and pull him back but I was not fast enough. Pedr swung himself onto the horse's back and pulled his sword and scabbard from beneath the riding rug. He slung the swordbelt over his shoulder and dug his heels into the animal. I was stricken by unbelief in the nightmare that was unfolding before my eyes. Pedr, my friend, was riding out to *DIE*.

It was Paulus who released me from the spell. 'Is he dying for nothing? What do we do?'

'Let's go!' I said and helped him hurriedly over to the other horse, Paulus's Cadfan. I helped him onto the animal's back and then mounted behind him. I took out our swords from beneath the rugs with a struggle and put his over his shoulder. Then we drew our blades. I held the reins over Paulus's head and we clattered out of the courtyard and through the open gate. Now Pedr was in view again, shouting and waving his sword as he galloped like a man possessed up the track way towards the Saxons who seemed vastly surprised. Then, as he reached to within a spear's length of them he turned the horse sharply to the left and was off obliquely down the bank of the hollow. The Saxons followed shouting oaths and war-cries. We set off as fast as the horse would carry the two of us up the track. At the top, we paused and looked back. They rushed him on all sides. He yelled ferociously, a man possessed, and the horse carried him straight into a group of them who charged in his path. The horse trampled some down and the whirling blade cut through them like a knife through cheese . . . then the impetus of his charge failed and the horse stumbled on the bodies of the Saxons. I saw six broad blades slash and sink into Pedr's belly, the look of torment and the almost, almost triumphant scream that issued and re-echoed from his contorted mouth.

'Pedr!' I yelled. 'PEDRRRRRRRR – ' Paulus struck me with his fist, shaking me out of the hysterical shout. Hot tears rolled unchecked down my cheek and tasted salty on my lips. Paulus wept also, but he was never as close to Pedr as I. We galloped, anger like a dragon in my breast, away from the hollow and towards the west.

We rode all day in a kind of daze. I could not accept that Pedr was *DEAD*, his body unmoving, his heart not beating and thoughts no longer in his mind. No more to hear his joking, or to hunt the boar at his side. I kept half turning to see if he was following and then the memory of his death suddenly came to me again and again and again. It was as if a piece had been cut from my body; half of me was missing.

We camped that night beneath a clear sky with the leaves of an ash rustling above our heads. It was lucky that night was not cold as we had left the bulk of our furs back at the villa. It was stupid to make camp here, just east of the road with the Saxons rampaging not far behind, but neither of us cared. Life seemed suddenly unprecious now that Pedr had given up his own. I wondered what sort of after-life he was enjoying, I never knew for sure which god or gods he worshipped.

When I slept, I dreamt that Pedr returned to us in the morning alive and well after a miraculous escape from the jaws of the Sea Wolves. But he was dead for sure, and I woke up crying like a child. There was nothing else to do . . . nothing more I could do. Pedr had given us the chance to live, and we could not return the gift.

CHAPTER NINE

Homecoming

The rock on which Ceorl's camp stood was an ugly protuberance on the landscape. We approached at midday as the sun was high in the sky, though the light it shed was pale and the sky was like milk floating in water.

It was not as I expected. The camp was not deserted for I could see the guards patrolling the defences. On three sides, the rock was supported by banks which were dense with trees. The front of the rock was bare and the colour of rusty iron. The camp was entered and exited by two trackways, the one on the side of the hill opposite the rock side and the other adjacent to the rock face on a thinly forested section of the bank rising steeply to our left until it reached the flat top of the camp, which was in turn enclosed by the ramparts. As we drew nearer we could see the tops of the huts peering over the fences.

We approached by the track which led to the main entrance of the encampment on the thinly forested slope. The last journey had done Paulus's wound no good and he was finding it nearly impossible to stand on his own feet. I had to hold him on the back of the horse and at the same time control the animal at a fast pace in case we were caught up by the Saxons or Paulus would have fallen from the horse and perhaps reopen the wound.

It was the fact that the Saxons were not far behind that made me surprised to see the fort was manned by about twenty of Ceorl's men. They must have known the Saxons were coming because of the flow of refugees from the east. What surprised me even more as we entered the encampment was the presence of Ceorl himself walking around looking over the defences. I couldn't think why he had not fled with those of his men who must have gone to the western lands.

I went to the picket-lines, leading the horse with Paulus seated on him and found that there were no other horses in the camp. I tethered Cadfan to the peg and helped Paulus down from his back. The next problem was to find some food and some shelter.

The huts of the camp were deserted by families and

occupied only by the remaining men of the camp. We found a place in one of the smaller huts and there I left Paulus sitting weakly on the reed matting whilst I wandered around to see what I could pick up in the way of food. We had not eaten since before we had arrived at the villa. I found some scraps of bread in a hut which was empty but for someone's belongings. These crusts I took back to Paulus and we ate them along with some raw meat which he had scrounged from one of the other men in the hut.

There were no women at all in the camp. Eiluned was not here. In fact I never saw Eiluned again, nor Aonghus, Peneli or Elspeth. I often wonder what became of them; I will for as long as I live I suppose.

There was still hope in my heart as I walked around the camp late that afternoon whilst Paulus slept through the weakness induced by the wound. I spoke to no-one, just walked around looking over the encampment as though I had been away from it for years on end.

When darkness closed around the camp, Paulus woke and asked me to help him to walk outside for a breath of fresh air. We went to the defences and looked out over the surrounding countryside. We stood there for a long time without saying anything, just leaning against the fence and surveying the landscape. Then we heard someone coming behind us. It was Ceorl. I would rather he hadn't been there, his company made me nervous and wakened old memories. 'Why are *YOU* wearing a sword, Rhydwyn?' he asked.

'Times have changed, Ceorl,' I replied.

'We were at Camboglanna,' Paulus added.

Ceorl stepped between us and leaned on the fence. He looked at me. 'Where's your friend, Pedr?'

'Dead,' I answered simply, not wishing to give details. 'We ran into some Saxons. You'll have to move soon, the Saxons'll be here in a few days time.'

'I'm not moving,' Ceorl said, turning back to look out of the camp.

'Why not?' asked Paulus.

'Because I don't wish to,' Ceorl said. 'Those who wanted to leave have gone.'

'Did they take the horses?' I enquired.

'No.'

'Where are the horses, then?' Paulus asked him.

'Some ten men went out to see how close the Saxons are. They haven't returned yet, but they will.'

'What're you going to do when the Saxons arrive?' I asked.

'Kill a few,' Ceorl replied, seeming not to care. He stood up and began to walk away. Then he turned and said, 'You two staying or leaving?' We both shrugged and he merely walked away to the longhut.

'What do you plan to do?' I asked Paulus after a pause.

'Don't know. What do you think our chances are if we stay here?'

'That depends on how many Saxons are on their way in this general direction,' I answered. 'Ceorl doesn't seem to care either way.'

'Are you?'

'I'm not sure. There doesn't seem a great deal to do apart from just living or dying, if you see what I mean.'

Paulus thought for a moment. 'I suppose that's what Pedr believed.'

For myself, I don't really know what drove him to do what he did for us. Pedr had been the most *ALIVE* person among my friends, and yet he rode out of that courtyard headlong into the abyss of death. I choose not to ponder too long on his death, the memory of his life is better kept.

The next day saw the return of Ceorl's horsemen, among them Walwyn. The thing I noticed first about him as he rode by me, the hooves of his horse squelching in the mud, was the crooked scar on his left cheek which I guessed was the remnant of the mutilation caused by the horse trampling on his face when we encountered him along with five others in Ceorl's ambush. He avoided my gaze, and Paulus's too, who was standing leaning on a stick next to me near the main gate. I tried to put an apology into my eyes, but my eyes I could never control. Perhaps I ought to try to conceal my thoughts as Wenda did.

The leader of the squadron of horses gave his horse over to another man and hurried into the longhut where Ceorl awaited his report. A crowd of people gathered outside the hut also waiting to hear the news. I didn't see what difference it could make to them since they all had chosen to remain at the camp anyway, but then I could not see that then because of my own confused images of life and death.

I went over to the picket-lines where the horses were being tied up by their riders, Paulus clinging to my shoulder with one hand and manipulating the stick with the other. I saw Walwyn's characteristic dark features moving around one of the horses. 'Hello, Walwyn,' I said.

'Hello,' Walwyn responded in his far-off voice and then continued to busy himself with the horse.

'What's the situation like?' I asked, trying to make conversation.

'The whole area's crawling with Saxons.' He came from behind the horse and stood in front of me. His face had once been handsome, but the angry red scar chewed at his bronzed skin and distorted the way in which his proud moustache grew.

'Separate war-bands?' Paulus asked.

'Up to now,' Walwyn answered. His left eye twitched and I noticed other smaller scars about his nose and eyes. The scar must have irritated him. He gazed over the camp to the east and looked out at the landscape I had found so fascinating, despite the fact that it was so familiar. I could see his face in profile now. The nose was broken, but not badly. 'If the Saxons unite we stand no chance sitting here in this camp.'

'Are you leaving, then?' Paulus asked him.

'I'd like to, but the others are staying. I said I'd stay when Ceorl asked us.' He rubbed the scar, scratched it, flinched and rubbed it again.

'Sorry about that,' I apologised, nodding towards his face. He touched it with his finger.

'That's alright, I'll live. I'll live until a united army of Saxons attack this camp. Then . . . well you may see that for yourselves.'

'We aren't absolutely sure that we're staying,' Paulus hastened to say.

We walked slowly beside Walwyn to join the crowd outside the longhut who waited for Ceorl to tell them what the situation was. We didn't have to wait long; Ceorl didn't talk for any great length of time about anything. When he came out, the crowd hushed and pushed to move in closer. He made no effort to console the people, or even raise his voice so that every man could hear. 'They're coming this way. A large number of them. If you feel like dying you'll do as you agreed and stay here.' And then he went back into the longhut again. That was the last we heard from him on the Saxons until the time came when we could learn what we needed to know with our eyes and our noses.

That night Paulus and I stood at the defences again. We could not discuss whether or not we were going to stay at Ceorl's camp with the other men around who shared the hut. Paulus told me that he would make his decision on the basis of my own, which did not please me as I didn't want him to risk his own life on my account. But it was his choice to follow my example, so I couldn't alter his mind whatever conclusion I reached. He had shown his obstinacy before. 'I'm staying, Paulus,' I told him. It had been nagging at the back of my mind since we arrived that I was destined to remain here and fight alongside the rest of them.

'I'll stay too,' Paulus said. I knew he would and felt slightly guilty. But I made myself realise that though Paulus was smaller than I he was as much a man as he'd ever be. I hope that I was right in thinking that.

'We went a long way around just to come home to this camp, Paulus,' I said to him.

Paulus sighed heavily. 'It cost us dear, nearly all we had.'

I agreed with that, though not in the material sense that Paulus meant. Not only had we lost a dear friend and all that made us more than poor, I had lost my previous self. Only a little remained of Ailin Rhydwyn the quiet blacksmith, the warrior without a sword; now I was Ailin Rhydwyn, the follower of a cause with death in and on my body. I had died, and was now reincarnated in another self. I think that I must hate myself now for I am no longer at peace. I no longer have honour, nor do I believe in myself, which is just about as low as you can sink when you betray that fundamental good in your character; that sweet essence everyone possesses, no matter how small and hidden.

The next morning, I went out of the encampment, down the track on which we had found the Saxon lying and walked to the bottom of the slope. I went straight ahead until I came to a ditch in the bottom of which flowed a tiny stream of golden water that babbled over the slimy pebbles on the bottom. For no reason at all, I followed the stream to its source, where it emerged from a spring not far from the encampment hill. Here the water was deeper and the presence of water plants made the bottom darker. Here I could peer into the water and see the face of Ailin Rhydwyn. It was a long time since I had bothered to examine my reflection. It was pretty much the same as ever. The hair was longer, I had not bothered to maintain my Roman-style haircut. I still shaved but not so regularly as I had done so in the past and there were grey bristles around my chin and cheeks and beneath my nose which seemed rather too small for the vast, broken expanse of my face. And my eyes, my eyes which betrayed the secrets of my heart to all but me, to whom they seemed impenetrable. Then the sky, reflected in the spring, grew dark and rain began to fall. I returned to the camp and stayed in the hut for most of the time until late afternoon.

As the sun was westering, I left the hut with Paulus to exercise his cramped legs. We found Walwyn sitting on a tree-stump greasing the blade of his sword. We talked for a while and then returned to the hut. There was little to do, and the men in the camp were already sick of waiting for the enemy to arrive.

We waited for three more days before they did finally come. We spent that time hunting, with little success, and wandering aimlessly around the defences. When they did finally arrive, we wished that we could have waited somewhat longer.

CHAPTER TEN

The Burden that is Life

The first group of the Saxons to see the encampment attempted to attack from the rear, coming up the trackway which led to the rear gateway. I went with the others on the horses. We rushed them as they came up the trackway. They made the mistake of trying to run from our onslaught and the trackway was strewn with their bodies. Their bodies were soon naked and bloody after we had stripped them of their furs and their weapons.

Paulus was glad of the extra warmth during the night which followed the massacre of the war-band. I hoped they would continue to attack in such small bands so as to not put too much pressure on our defences. But I knew we would soon have to face a greater trial. The Saxons we slaughtered on the track were mostly young men, with only the lust for booty and glory in their hearts. They had been foolish and had answered with their lives. The older ones, who probably regarded such camps as ours as the most minor of obstacles, would follow. How far behind other Saxons were no-one knew. We only hunted close to home and that was all. I no longer walked alone outside the camp for fear of a surprise attack which could come any time. I recalled the Saxons emerging from the forest at the villa. It served as a lesson to me.

Paulus could not get about successfully without my assistance. It seemed that the wound in his side would never heal altogether. I think that Paulus expected the same. He became less willing to talk, except when he was asking for reassurance that the wound would clear up eventually. I always gave him that reassurance, though I myself was doubtful.

The defences suffered a lot more in the next attack. This time the rush came on both sides, at both gateways. We lost four men and others were wounded. There were more Saxons involved in this attack, but they gave up after losing ten of their number and continued on their way west, leaving us to our burials.

During the attack most of the enemy dead had met their ends within the confines of the camp's defences. This caused me some worry as Paulus was so vulnerable with his wound still giving him a rough time.

The attack which we feared followed after four days. There were something like a hundred Saxon warriors advancing towards us. They probably didn't know we existed as they moved closer to us during those four days. But we knew that *THEY* were coming; we were expecting them to come.

I watched with Paulus hanging onto my shoulder and Walwyn next to him from the fence as the weapons of the enemy gleamed in the sunlight signalling their advance towards the camp.

'I feel the way I felt when we saw the Saxons coming at the villa,' Paulus remarked.

'You mean you feel that death is waiting for us to come very soon? I feel that way too,' I told him. At any other time I would have given him hope for survival, but at this moment there seemed no hope but to run, to escape as we did when Pedr was killed. Neither of us wanted to run any more, to let other men die in our place.

'It seems to me that death is coming to us,' Walwyn said, not taking his gaze from the oncoming Saxons. Men from all over the camp flocked to the defences to watch the enemy coming.

We spoke in quiet tones, not wanting to raise our voices for some reason. I thought it would be well to meet my final end in the sunlight as this day was sunny indeed. 'It won't be like Camboglanna,' I said to Paulus who took his weight from my shoulder and transferred it to the fence.

'No,' he agreed, 'In this battle we will not have our horses to afford us protection. I wonder how I will fare in the fight. I will be of little value to the others with this wound in my side.'

Suddenly I feared for him again. How horrible to be killed whilst lying on your back or being incapable of offering any kind of defence against your assailant.

'I'll stay here to meet the Saxons,' Paulus said.

'I think not, old friend. You can take cover in one of the storage pits. You'll stand a better chance in a confined space,' I said.

Paulus turned to me. 'Who needs a chance? I'd rather have it quickly.'

'We are too morbid,' I said to him. 'Let's at least fight until the last possible heartbeat. Think of how Pedr died and let the anger out of your system when the Saxons finally trap you.'

'We may live on,' Walwyn said. He didn't mean it, but he needed to say so because he wasn't as used to the idea of dying as Paulus and I had become.

By now the enemy was close. We could hear their voices faintly now. They sounded joyful, full of the fruits of victory. It was so unlike the atmosphere at Camboglanna. The sun was shining and the day was so unfit for a battle. Men should not die so when the sun shines. Death is a dark thing for rain and storm, I thought. But I no longer cared about the way in which my own final destiny would be reached, I was more concerned for my friend. I took hold of his arm. 'The storage pit,' I told him and I led him away from the defences to the nearest pit. I lowered the ladder, which lay nearby, and helped him to struggle down into the almost empty hole. There were a couple of bags of grain and these I used to prop him up with. He drew his sword and sat to wait for the attack. I left him and returned to the surface. The pit was without a cover, so I took one from one of the other storage pits and put it over the hole which contained Paulus though he protested.

When I returned to Walwyn, the enemy had gained ground and their cries were a lot louder and the features of the host more distinct. We could see men pointing up to the camp and talking amongst themselves.

I left the defences and went to the horses. Men were already mounting the animals, which stamped the earth and snorted, the way the horses had waited for the charge at Camboglanna. The horses were never this way when we prepared for a hunting trip; it was as if they knew that today was a day for killing.

Soon after I had mounted, Ceorl came up and mounted too whilst one of the men steadied the horse for him. He looked at one of the other horsemen. 'Tell the bowmen to concentrate on the main entrance, we'll cover the rear.' The man rode to the defences and shifted all the bowmen to the vicinity of the main gate.

We followed Ceorl to the rear entrance and stood there, firmly waiting for a sight of the enemy coming up the winding track. We had not long to wait before we saw the sun flashing on their spears and swords as they began to accumulate near the bottom of the hill. It was difficult to see with the trees in the way and I thought that might make the charge difficult too. If these were experienced, as their very trend to unity seemed to suggest, then few of these men would follow the easy route up the hill by the trackway. They would keep to the trees to hinder the horses.

After a short while the jangle of the Saxons started to get closer. We caught brief glimpses of them coming up through the trees. I drew my sword slowly and noiselessly and the others did the same. As the enemy drew closer to the first bend in the track, Ceorl raised his sword above his head. We knew that when his blade fell it would be time to charge.

I don't know whether or not the Saxons knew we were waiting before we actually charged. The way it turned out, the element of surprise made little difference.

As the first of them rounded the bend, Ceorl gave a shout and started them off down the trackway. We all followed and I thought of Camboglanna and the way it'd been there. But the memories didn't last long. I followed a group up the forested slope to the left and we searched in among the trees for the enemy. I caught sight of one of them and started towards him. He kept coming and avoided me at the last moment in a bid to reach the top. My horse's hooves skidded in the leaves strewn on the ground and I was on my way uphill after him. When I was almost upon him, he turned just in time to see my blade fall to cut into his skull.

I started over towards the trackway again. Here we regrouped and reawaited Ceorl's signal. In no time we were careering downhill again. I broke off to the left again, but I was astonished to see Ceorl leading the others further and further down the track. Suddenly there was a clashing of arms and shouting. I rushed back onto the track to get a better view. Men had descended from all around onto the horsemen. They were completely surrounded and one by one they went down. There was nothing I could do. Ceorl had led them into the thick of it for some insane reason and they all died. I turned and galloped back to the camp.

At the camp, the defences were failing to withstand the Saxons. The enemy seethed over like fire licking at an ember, and blood spilled all around. One of the huts caught fire and the smoke choked the air. The noise drummed on my ears. Then through the confusion I saw Walwyn's head fall from his body in a crimson flash and I remembered Paulus.

I galloped around the cluster of huts to the other side of the camp where the storage pit was. When I reached it, I dismounted and stooped to draw back the cover slightly. Paulus stared up at me, still in the position I had left him. Then he shouted suddenly; 'Look out!' and I fell into the pit. I saw a massive golden-haired Saxon glaring down at me. He threw his spear. It missed me and I thrust my sword up and into his heart. He fell with a clatter to cover the opening between the edge of the cover and the side of the pit. I turned to Paulus.

'That was clo – – – ' Paulus had a spear through his neck. The blood flowed down his tunic onto the sacks of grain. His blood was everywhere. His frightened eyes rolled, he tried to speak but only blood came. Then he died. 'Paulus! Paulus!' I grabbed him and held him close to my breast and the warm blood covered me and flowed and flowed. . . . And I cried again, for the last time as the battle raged above me I nursed Paulus and cried. He was . . . dead.

EPILOGUE

I rode out of Ceorl's camp after I had buried Paulus. There was no-one else alive, but I had been saved, hiding in the grain-pit. There were no Saxons, now; they had gone on their way after finding little booty.

I took the only surviving horse, even though it was lame, and left by the path on which we had found Aonghus a thousand years ago. I wondered then if Pedr and Paulus would be dead if we had not found him. The question was complicated and I soon forgot it.

I was still alive, in a way. I wondered if I should be thankful for that, because I was not. Inside I was dead.

I am still riding now. Nobody knows nor cares for my story or my sorrow. There must be others throughout the land with similar loss. The events of this year have shown me that gods who boast mercy, wisdom and love show none whether it is my own god or that of the Christians or those of the Saxons. The gods are without mercy, without substance. I am without substance in my mind. This is a land and a time without mercy, a land ruined by war and the hand of man. It is I who make it so for myself by my very presence in the land. I am not a hero, nor a coward, nor am I happy or sad. I simply ride on my luckless travels. I have reached an anti-climax in my life. It seems it is all over though I am barely past my twentieth year, and sorrow waits for each man in the bones of the earth. I cannot live nor die in this land.

NEL BESTSELLERS

NEL P.O. BOX 11, FALMOUTH, TR10 9EN, CORNWALL

Please send cheque or postal order. Allow 10p to cover postage and packing on one book plus 4p for each additional book.

Name ....

Address..

....

Title ....
(SEPTEMBER)